Maureen Tries Online Dating

A SENIORS' SCI-FI/ADVENTURE/HORROR NOVEL

Sherrill WARK

crowecreations.ca
Ottawa Canada

First Crowe Creations edition December 2021
crowecreations.ca

Designed by Crowe Creations
Text set in Times New Roman; headings set in Tempus Sans ITC

Cover photo from iStock: PeskyMonkey, Stock photo ID: 504680989
Cover design © 2021 by Crowe Creations

Crowe Creations
ISBN: 978-1-927058-86-2

To The Milers.

"Don't be afraid. Be very afraid."
—Veronica, *The Fly* (1986)

Prof. Henry Jarrod: [heavy with menace after Sue unwigs Cathy] You shouldn't have done that my dear!
—Vincent Price (as Prof. Henry Jarrod) in *House of Wax* (1953)

1

"**PICK UP. PICK** up. Dammit." Maureen stood on the edge of a deep earthen pit, one gnarled and ringless hand on a push handle of an occupied wheelchair, the other holding an open umbrella. She was wearing what she called her "hippy duds." Her shoes were "sensible sneakers."

In the wheelchair, an elderly man appeared to be sleeping. The umbrella covered her, not him. He was in excellent physical shape by the bulges in the arms of his expensive-looking, rain-wet shirt, and the absence of bulging belly. If his shirt had been any wetter, his abs would have shown, too. A broad-brimmed, black hat sat deeply on his head and the angle it was at, hid most of his face. Rainwater dripped off the hat, making a puddle between his long thighs as though he were incontinent. Water poured off his leather shoes. Beneath the wheelchair, rivulets of rainwater flowed in little wiggling streams into the pit, bringing with it, bits of soil and small stones.

Towering beside Maureen, like a Godzilla-sized flamingo peering

1

into the pit with her, was a bright-yellow construction excavator, water running out of its tucked-under bucket like drool. Its main cab was covered with tarpaulin. Around it were other construction machines and NO TRESPASSING signs.

"Ah. There you are. It's me. I was about to *NOT* give up on you. I need your help."

Maureen paused.

"I desperately need your help."

Pause.

"Do you still know how to run one of those big construction digger things?"

Pause.

"I'm just up the street. Where they're putting in that new building."

Pause.

"No. There's nobody here. Sandra. For God's sake, look out the window. It's pouring rain. There's nobody here."

Pause.

"C'mon. Grab a brolly, dress appropriately, and come up here. I need to get rid of a body."

Maureen winced and popped out one of her cell phone's earbuds.

"I'll explain when you get here. Hurry up." Maureen popped out the other earbud then tapped at the phone hanging off the lanyard around her neck. She sighed deeply, shook her head and said, "Shit."

2

TALL, MASCULINE SANDRA soon arrived wearing a bright-yellow, full-length, polyester raincoat complete with hood and reflective stripes. She looked like a cross between a traffic cop and a radioactive street-corner drug seller.

"Why didn't you wear something conspicuous?" asked Maureen.

"You told me to dress appropriately, so shut up. Is this him?" As she leaned down to look up into the face of the man in the wheelchair, Sandra pushed her hood back, revealing short white hair, olive skin, high cheekbones, and not as many wrinkles as one might expect on the face of a woman in the second half of her seventies who'd spent most of her life working construction. "Hi there." Her eyebrows met briefly, then she rose to her full height. She pointed her thumb at him in a question.

"Yup. Him. I need to uh…"

"You're asking me to help you bury this guy? Who is he? Where did he come from?" Her smile was not a sincere one. "You went fishing and came up with a barracuda again. Right?"

"No. It wasn't that site. It was the one where they supposedly match you with all that psychological bullshit. You know, the one where you answer all these questions?"

"All I know is, if you told the truth on those things, you'd probably fare better. What did he do? Did he try to sexually assault you?"

"The opposite."

Sandra laughed. "Your first date and you try to force yourself onto this…" She leaned down to look up into the man's face again. "Let me see. He looks to be about… What? Maybe sixty-five? … this *kid*?"

"Stop it. You know I don't like the old ones."

"I think you must have invented the cougar concept." Hands on hips, Sandra stood straight again and looked around at the construction site. "Lucky you. Not even a security guard."

"He's only ten years younger than I am."

"Twelve maybe? Thirteen?" She turned to Maureen. "So what happened? And why didn't you call 9-1-1? I'm assuming he had a heart attack or something. I thought you were a total fan of those forensics shows where they try to solve the crime within two days or something. You know how they all end up. Jailed for life, or even hanged if you're black. Lucky you, eh? White skin and ovaries. Such as they are anymore."

"I don't know what happened. He suddenly just went… Like he is right now."

"So why not call 9-1-1? You have nothing to hide."

Maureen's eyes went toward the pit.

"Or do you? Uh… Maureen? What did you do to him?"

"It wasn't our first date. We've met a few times. He's really smart. He's in great shape. He runs all the time. He dances at Arthur Murray's, for God's sake. Ka-ching, ka-ching. He's interesting. He's sexy as hell."

"So what's he need the wheelchair for?"

"That's mine, remember? Popped my hip out a few years ago?

Managed to snag a top-of-the-line chair for free by playing Pity Me?"

"I don't know how you get away with half the stuff you get away with."

"I kept it. Why not? I'll probably need it again eventually. Eventually, smart ass. Don't look at me like that. Maybe in twenty-five, thirty years."

"It's not his so that means you guys were playing nurse." Sandra laughed loudly but quickly brought her fingers to her mouth and glanced around. "Sorry. Gotta be quiet."

"I don't play nurse."

"Ah yes. That's right. Sorry. But here *I* am, driving these construction machines *my* whole life and you're expecting *me* to play construction guy? Just because we're friends? Working construction can be just as PTSD-inducing as ER nursing, y'know."

"Yeah, I know."

"How'd you get him into it, though? Guess he didn't fall on the floor. Not even Nurse Maureen could do that at her age."

"Lucky for me, he was in that dining room chair with the arms on it. So he just kind of slumped over."

"Ah, yes. The one I'm always banging my elbows on."

"We were having lunch."

"Uh huh."

"Wasn't easy to switch him from chair to chair, but... Years of nursing training, right?"

Sandra waited.

"You'll be happy to know I had to take the arms off that chair. And the arms of this thing fold down."

"I will do my best to help you out, but I won't make a move until you tell me exactly what happened. *Exactly* what happened."

A chunk of wet mud slid into the pit near Maureen's right sneaker. "I wanted to be with him."

"You mean *with him* with him?"

Maureen nodded.

"OK. So then you…"

"So then I… We were having a lovely glass of Napa Valley Sauvignon Blanc. Purchased and brought to me by him, by the way. See why I like him so much?"

"Go on."

"I decided to do something. Something I've thought about many times in the past but never had the guts to do."

"Continue."

"Do I have to?"

Sandra's eyes told her yes.

"I had put the bottle of wine in the fridge. When I went to refill our glasses, I…"

"Yes?"

"I snuck into the bedroom where I keep a supply of…"

"Yes?"

"… something in one of my jewelry boxes."

"Oh, I don't like the sound of this."

"You've heard of the little blue pill?"

"Oh, dear. And you put… What? Two or three into his glass? How many do they need at that age, anyway?" She stifled a giggle. "I have no clue. We gay gals don't need anything like that."

"Only one. No more than one. *Ever!* Those things can cause a lot of issues." One side of Maureen's mouth pinched itself into a non-smile. "Obviously, eh?" She shrugged. "He had no sooner taken two or three sips of wine and flop! Out he went."

Another chunk of soil slid away from the area near Maureen's foot. This time, the wheelchair moved, too.

Both women made a grab for it but it was too late.

An entire slab of soil, made wet by the day's heavy downpour, took all three of them down into the pit as gently as an iceberg might slide into the Antarctic Ocean—at least according to Facebook YouTube videos.

"Dammit," said Maureen.

"Ditto," said Sandra.

3

THE "EARTHEN PIT" the trio had just slid into was actually the
foundation of the City's latest building project, its latest subsidized-
housing apartment building. What could be called the "floor" was
smooth, flat concrete that had been stabbed to their hilts with perhaps
two dozen evenly spaced columns, also concrete. There would be more
pillars under the mud slide; they'd barely missed slamming into one on
the way down. Hanging like drapery against the left wall and touching
the floor, was a square of tarpaulin, about twelve feet by twelve feet.
The back wall and the opposite wall were bare except for blasting scars
on their faces. The heavy rain deadened any exterior sounds.

The wheelchair had arrived in an upright position at the bottom of
this huge, sloping mud slide. Maureen and Sandra were behind it with
their bums in the mud. The man, who still sat in the chair, had not
changed position whatsoever.

"How did we manage to do that?" asked Maureen, grimacing as she pulled her left hand out of the wet mud. It made a sucking sound as she did so. "Ew." Her right hand still held her umbrella upright and open.

The hood of Sandra's raincoat had slid off. She flipped it back onto her head, ignoring the sprinkles of water that came out of it to run down the back of her neck. "Shall we attribute our escape from certain death to the magic of Mary Poppins and her umbrella?"

"Huh?"

"Never mind. It was an attempt at humor." With very little complaining and groaning, Sandra managed to extricate herself from the mud to stand over Maureen, one hand extended to Maureen's free hand. "Come on. Up you get."

As Maureen reached to grasp Sandra's hand, she cried out. "Ow, ow. I think I put my hip out again. Shit."

"Oh, no. Does it hurt?"

"Does the Pope pardon pedophiles? Of course it hurts? Just a minute." Maureen handed the umbrella to Sandra. "Put that down for a sec." She flipped over onto hands and knees. Then, raising her body from the knees up, she reached out to grasp both of Sandra's hands. "Ready?"

"Ready."

With both eyes crushed closed and mouth pinched, Maureen slid her left leg forward so its foot would be firmly on the surface and its thigh, parallel to ground level.

"Now pull back."

Sandra pulled and Maureen's entire body was perpendicular.

"Ah. Thank you. There. Give me my umbrella. Sorry for that crack about the Pope."

Sandra shrugged. "It's not like I haven't heard that one before. Want me to close this thing up?"

"Uh. Yeah. Good idea."

Sandra closed the umbrella and handed it to Maureen who quickly settled it, cane-like, into her right hand. Maureen moved her right leg to the side and placed that foot onto the smooth concrete floor. "It's OK. I'm OK. Once I'm upright, I can usually manage to—" She moved her other leg to the level concrete floor. "—move properly. God, I hate it when I have to act my fucking age."

"You sure you're OK? That floor is wet. Careful."

Something made Maureen look up to where they had come from. She blinked the rain out of her eyes. "Uh… Sandra?"

"What?"

"Uh. You're the expert on like, uh, like construction machines and stuff, right?"

"Yeah." Sandra turned to look up at the top of the mud slide. "Reminds me of the old days when we used to slide down slopes like this. But it was snow."

"Yep. And with bullies waiting at the top of the hill then, too. Can you see that far?"

"Bullies? Nah. They just wanted you to notice them— Oh. Oh. No." Color drained out of the top of Sandra's cheeks.

From the top of the long slope of mud, the excavator's tracks peeked over.

"See what I mean?"

"Yeah."

"That thing's not going to stay there, is it?"

"How fast can you move?" Sandra snatched the umbrella-cane from Maureen and stabbed it into the wheelchair behind the man. "Grab onto the handles and let's go! I'm right behind you. I'll make sure you don't fall."

Within seconds, they were at the far wall and Sandra was helping Maureen turn the wheelchair around so both of them could have their backs against something solid and with some protection from the downpour. The wheelchair between them and potential death served only as mental comfort; it would not protect them from anything.

Their eyes were on the excavator as they watched the heavy rain wash away more and more soil, faster and faster, from under its tracks. A stone the size of a tangerine went rolling down the slope to bang against one of the pillars. From there, it ricocheted toward them and bounced off one of the wheelchair's foot supports, making the chair ding.

This made Sandra turn her face away and from this new angle, she could see behind the tarpaulin. There was space behind it, a section cut into the rock.

"I think we can get into a safer spot. Let's go." She grabbed the wheelchair and turned it to face the area behind the tarp. "See it? Go!"

Maureen grabbed the handles of the wheelchair again and waddled ahead as fast as her dislocated hip would allow.

"Go, go. Go. I got ya. I'm right behind you."

As they slid in behind the tarp hanging over the large open space there, a rumbling, chumbling, boinging told them the excavator's treads had finally let go and the excavator had succumbed to gravity. A mass of wet mud splooshed under the tarp, coming to within inches of their feet. They stepped back. Behind them, lights flickered on overhead.

"Once again, the gods appear to be with us, eh? Despite that crack about the Pope."

"That's not funny. I said I was sorry."

"You don't look so good. I think you better sit down."

Sandra offered her forearm and helped Maureen make her way to a bench on the other side of the space.

The space was a tunnel. Its floor was flat. Against the wall opposite from where Maureen sat were the fridge Sandra was now rooting through; steel shelves with construction helmets, boots, drills, lamps, flashlights, and gadgets most people couldn't put names to; and beside the shelves was a closed cabinet whose lock was unsnapped and hanging there.

"This is weird," said Sandra. "I've never known of any company digging a sideways tunnel out from a foundation before. I've got a feeling it goes way back. Lights. Echoes. Look."

Maureen looked.

A bottle of water in each hand, Sandra turned to Maureen. "We have two options. Scream and be saved." She gave one of the bottles to Maureen. "Or look for a way out. I say scream."

"Did you forget our, uh, dead body here?"

"*Our* dead body? He ain't my dead body, girl. He's all yours."

"I'll phone my niece. She'll… Uh…" Maureen patted her substantial bosom then pulled the neck of her dress out to look inside. "I seem to have lost my cell."

Sandra shook her head in mock sympathy. "Gone but not forever, right? According to those shows you like, somebody will find it. They'll hand it over to the detectives. Then some expert or other will look through it and learn that you and your boyfriend here were hooking up. They're gonna get you before the first two or three hours are up, never mind forty-eight."

"Oh stop. I know." She reached for her ears. "My bud things are gone, too."

"And your ear wax'll be on those. Full of DNA." She faked an evil laugh. "You're doomed, my friend. Doomed."

"That's not funny. We have to get out of—"

Along with the noise of the pounding rain, voices trickled down from above. One was cop-like. The other was gravelly and slurred as though from someone "familiar to police."

"Jerome. Come on. I don't have time to be messing around. What's this now? The third time you've called this week? Monday it was a UFO?"

"I'm tellin' ya, Officer. I seen two old ladies standing right there."

Old ladies? Maureen mouthed to Sandra. "Bastard."

"Shhh. Listen."

"Just before that dang digger went slidin' down. They had a guy tied up in a wheelchair."

Tied up? This time, Sandra was the one mouthing the question.

"Jerome…"

"Honest to Christ and on my mother's grave, Officer. I seen them. They was standing there. Right there. One of them was dressed up in a long dress with crazy colored swishes all over it. The other one was dressed up like a cop."

"A cop."

"Like a cop directing traffic when it rains."

"So this person you think you saw was wearing rain gear, then."

"I didn't *think* I seen her. I did see her."

"How do you know it was female if they were all covered up?"

"Cuz like I uh…"

"Jerome? Do I have to take you downtown? Want to go through detox?"

"No, no, no. I'm telling the truth. I uh… I uh… I went to the edge of the construction area here. Before the digger went down. I seen them. Down at the bottom of the mud slide. I used to slide down them things when I was a kid. Did you?"

"No, I did not."

"But I mean when they was made out of snow."

"Jerome."

"Oh. Yeah. Sorry. So I seen the two old ladies sitting down at the bottom of the mudslide and their prisoner was still sitting in the wheelchair."

Prisoner? Both women's mouths formed the word.

"And you saw this how?"

"I was sleeping behind the dumpster." A pause. "I heard one of them talking to herself. She probably has that schizo thing there when they hear voices? You know about that?"

"All too well, Jerome. And?"

"Well then another one showed up and her voice was a woman's voice. Oh, wait. I guess that's how come I knew it was a woman. It was kind of a dykey voice, but a woman's just the same. I can always tell if it's a woman." A stifled giggle floated down to the tunnel entrance. The rain was easing. "They got titties."

"So, you were standing on the edge of this and you didn't fall in, too?"

"I'm surprisingly nimble on my feet, Officer. See?"

This pause was interrupted by another man's voice.

"Dammit. Dammit. Dammit. I told him. I told him. I don't know how many times I told him to back that thing away from the goddamned edge of the foundation. Hey. Tom. How're doing?"

A mumble.

"And Jerome. Do I have to tell you, yet again, to stay the hell off our property?"

"There's two ladies and their prisoner down in your basement. I seen them. I seen them push him over and then they slid in and then the digger went in."

"Is that right, eh? Did you hear that, Officer?"

A mumble.

Maureen and Sandra had been peering out through the slit where the tarp and wall almost met so were able to see a silhouette of the shoulders and helmeted head of a man leaning over to look down.

"I've got men on the way, Officer. You can leave it to me now. Just get him out of here."

Another head, this one's silhouette with long hair, appeared beside him.

"Hey. Hey. Not too close, eh? Jeez. Get him out of here."

The officer's voice said, "Jerome. Come on."

Jerome said, "Them ladies didn't go down there on purpose. I'm sure of that. I think they were here to toss that poor bugger down there. Kill him, you know? And Karma got them." He giggled again. "Hope it doesn't find out where I live. Er, where I don't live." He guffawed. "See? There are benefits to being homeless."

"Jerome. Come on. Let's go."

The figures disappeared from the edge of the opening.

"That means only one option is available now," said Maureen. "We have to see how far this tunnel goes and where it ends up."

4

"WHERE'S YOUR PHONE?"

"At home. Charging. Why?"

"I want to Google Ottawa tunnels. There used to be tunnels under Ottawa. Did you know that?"

"I worked construction, remember?"

"So it's true then?" Maureen was once again seated on the bench. "Was this maybe one of them?"

"Could be. This is sort of what they look like. Although…" Sandra's eyes searched the ceiling and walls. "This part is new…"

"All right. Here's the plan. We'll load up on… How much water's in the fridge? Is there any food?"

"Enough. We'll need flashlights." Sandra went to the closed cabinet and opened it. A blast of light made her face glow. She leaned in. "Woo! They're all charged up. Yesss." She pumped her fist at shoulder level.

"Aren't they using up the batteries leaving the lights on like that?"

Sandra rummaged around inside the cabinet and, piling one arm up with flashlights, she headed for the wheelchair. "Give me a hand. Turn these off and stick them into the pockets. Look at all the pockets this thing has. Wow. I can't believe this wheelchair. I'm surprised it doesn't have its own jet engine or something."

"I took the motor off." At Sandra's frown she explained, "Forgot to plug in the battery."

Sandra continued to frown.

"It's heavy. He's heavy. I lightened the load. Give me a break." She flipped one of the flashlights around and up and down until she found the off switch. "What's this funny-looking thingy on the top."

"Solar panel. They can charge each other when their lights are on." Sandra placed one of the big flashlights between the legs of the man on the wheelchair. Its light spread out in a bright circle creating tiny slits of shadow that streaked the walls, ceiling and floor. "I just found that out last week."

"Maybe someday they'll invent solar panels for us and stick them on our foreheads, eh?"

"Don't wish for that or they will."

Maureen laughed. "Remember those movies they used to have back in our day? With all the mind control and everything? Invaders from Mars sticking things into people's brains?"

"Yup. And giant spiders coming out of tunnels."

"Oh, God. Don't say spiders."

They finished filling up the wheelchair's pockets with flashlights, water and food. Sandra pushed a toolbox in beside the man's thigh on one side and more bottles of water on the other. Maureen's umbrella would continue to serve as her cane. She looped her purse over the man's neck to rest in his lap.

"There. All set?"

"All set." Sandra pushed the wheelchair forward.

☺

They'd been walking for perhaps fifteen minutes when they came to where the string of motion-sensor lights above them ended and the tunnel took a sharp curve to the right.

Sandra turned the wheelchair so its on-board flashlight would point down the tunnel. "It keeps going for as far as the flashlight reaches. But look at this." She turned the wheelchair slightly so its light would shine on a large, round, wooden door partway down the tunnel.

The door, plastered with warning stickers, painted-on symbols, and stapled signs and crisscrossing yellow ribbons with DANGER and CAUTION all along their lengths, seemed to dare them to open it.

"Is it locked?" asked Maureen, leaning forward with both hands on her makeshift cane. "Nobody'll follow us in there. It's against the law. Right?" She laughed. "Canadians are so obedient." She laughed again. "Generally speaking."

Sandra was examining the edges of the door. "No locks that I can see. You sure you want me to open this?"

"Duh."

"Some of these symbols look familiar to me, but I can't place them." Sandra ran her fingers over the sticker of a white skull with black around the eyes. "Looks like a pirate thing but I thought they all had crossed bones below them."

"I can't remember." Maureen moved closer and pointed to a tiny silver crucifix with its chain hanging from a nail the size of a railroad spike. She pointed to the figure on it. "This guy doesn't look like Jesus. It doesn't even have a body." She squinted. "Just a… a weird, round head on a cross. And a bunch of doodad things. How about you? Can you see what's on it?"

"Don't have my magnifying glass with me."

Maureen laughed.

"So now she laughs at something I've said. But that wasn't a joke."

"Do you actually use one of those?"

"Ever try to read the ingredients on a medicine bottle?"

"True enough."

"You OK?"

Maureen shifted again on her umbrella-cane. "My hip could use a rest."

"Let's give this a try then."

It took both Sandra and Maureen—with Maureen adding swear words—to get the wooden door pushed open far enough to allow the wheelchair to slide past it. And they had to undo the DANGER ribbon to accomplish this.

5

"GLAD WE BROUGHT all these flashlights with us, eh?"

A draft from somewhere inside the cylindrical tunnel that rose another two feet above their heads caused the big wooden door to hiss closed behind them.

"I don't know if I like this idea, Maureen."

"There's one."

Sandra jumped. "One what?"

"Chair. There's a chair. Up ahead. See? At the turn up there. Looks like maybe two chairs. Come on."

"You creep me out sometimes, my friend."

"Creep out? Why? I go by my instincts. That's all. Sorry I scared ya."

"I shouldn't have remembered that movie about giant spiders in tunnels."

"Sandra! This guy here isn't going to be the only one dead if you keep talking about spiders!"

"Then stop creeping me out by knowing stuff ahead of time." Sandra helped get Maureen settled onto one chair and she sat on the other one. "I'm surprised it's not dusty in here. It's almost like… Ixnay on that thought, too. I don't want to go there either. Change of subject. Tell me more about this dude."

"His online profile name is studmuffin57." Maureen's voice whispered away around the curving stone-walled tunnel with nary an echo.

Sandra laughed. "Seriously?"

"Seriously. Can you believe that? And I can't remember exactly how he said it, but his profile indicated…" Maureen snickered. "… that he had something… I think he used the word 'happy' or 'make her happy' or something like that. Know what I mean?"

"Yeah, I get it." Sandra was still laughing. "He probably has a… Hey. Remember that guy? There was a guy lived in… I think it was Shaw Falls, and they said… Like this guy wasn't very tall? Like just a little skinny guy? But he had a big… You know. A big… thing."

Now Maureen was laughing. "I remember that story. And they said every time he got a boner, he passed out."

"Maybe that's what happened to Mister Studmuffin here."

"He said I could call him Muffy."

"He wouldn't give you his real name? That sounds rather suspicious, don't you think?"

Maureen frowned. "I wonder if he has a phone on him."

Sandra glanced over at Muffy. "I'm not an avid fan of the stuff you like to read about and watch on TV, and I'm not a nurse like you were, but aren't they supposed to get all pale when they're sitting up dead like that? Like, there's nothing pumping the blood around so it settles?" With one arm stretched as far as it would stretch, Sandra poked his shoulder with her index finger. "And aren't they supposed to get stiff?"

"What?"

"I said—"

"I know what you said." Maureen rose to her feet. "It's too early for rigor to have established itself yet, but it should have at least maybe started." She poked the man's opposite shoulder then squeezed his forearm. Her fingers went immediately to the inside of his wrist. "Holy shit. He's not dead. Shit. Skin's not even cool. No pulse, though."

"How can that be? He's not doing anything. He's not breathing. He hasn't moved. Yeah, maybe he's got a phone. Find it. Call 9-1-1."

Maureen set her umbrella-cane aside and reached into the breast pocket of Muffy's shirt, then, tilting him over somewhat, she dug her hand into the side pocket of his dress pants and brought out a tiny pillbox that she handed to Sandra. Then she reached in again and came out with a small spray container. She did the same on the other side, then into a back pocket and came out with his cell phone.

"Never mind the phone for now." She set it on the man's thigh. "What's in that little spray container? I think I know but I don't want to."

Sandra was holding it with barely the ends of thumb and finger. She squinted. "It says ni-tro-gly-cer-in. Nitroglycerin. I'm not a doctor or anything but isn't that supposed to be for if you're having a heart attack or something?"

"It is and it does not get along with Viagra. At all!"

Sandra shook it then tapped the spray button. Nothing happened. "Empty."

"No. Don't tell me that. I don't want to know what's in the pillbox either, but I have to know. Tell me."

Sandra opened the hinged lid to reveal two small, blue, sideways-diamond-shaped pills.

"Oh my God. What if he already took one before I gave him one of mine? Is there anything written on those?"

With the tips of her fingers, Sandra picked one up and turned it this way and that way. "I can't see anything. But that doesn't mean there's nothing there."

Maureen took the pill from Sandra.

"Blank. The real ones have stuff written on them. I think. Here. I'll check." She handed the pill back to Sandra then dug into her purse that was still hanging around Muffy's neck. From it, she pulled out a prescription bottle then popped its lid off. She dumped part of the contents of the small plastic bottle onto her hand. She brought that hand close to her face and poked through the pile. "We're in trouble. His are fake. Probably got them from some drug dealer or something."

"What does that mean? And how could you get a prescription for that stuff?"

"Don't ask. Combine nitroglycerin with a street drug in the first place and then add one of mine and…" Maureen replaced the little blue pills into their plastic bottle, secured its lid and put it back into her purse. "Then add wine to that and we are in real deep trouble indeed."

"What's with this 'we'?"

"We're going to— I'm going to have to take a chance and call 9-1-1. But if you do it, they probably won't charge you as an accomplice."

"The word probably is supposed to make me feel good?"

Maureen lifted the cell phone from Muffy's thigh. She poked at it. "Dammit." She leaned over, holding the cell phone in front of Muffy. "Grab one of his fingers and poke his phone. Right there." She pointed at the Home button.

"No way, man! I'm not touching him."

"You already did. You touched his shoulder."

"Yeah, with my finger on his shirt. I'm not touching his hand. That's like real flesh. Are you nuts?"

"Well, here then. You hold the phone and I'll do the poking. You OK with that?"

Maureen handed the phone to Sandra who grimaced as she held it out in front of the man. Maureen placed one of the man's fingers on the Home button. The phone reacted.

"Awesome." She handed the phone to Sandra. "Phone 9-1-1."

"Oh. Wait. Looks like he's got a text here." Sandra smiled up at Maureen.

"What's it say?"

"It says, 'You bleep bleeping bleeper—'"

"Gimme that." Maureen took the phone from Sandra. "It says…" She laughed. "It says, 'You mother ducking bastion. I know what you've been doing. I've known for two years now. You obviously have no respect for me and the children.'"

"Sounds like a wife?"

"His profile says he's a widower."

"So he *is* a mother ducking bastion, then." Sandra laughed. "You sure can pick 'em, girl."

"Oh, wait. And she goes on to say that she… *She* is the one who switched out his little blue pills. She says she caught onto his bull shift—don't you love autocorrect, eh?—his bull shift noon-bowling-with-the-boys scam. Sounds a tad ticked?"

"What else does she say?"

"She says she's been keeping track of his pills since Christmas and she knows he's not been using them for her. So last week she found somebody who had some pills that look like his little blue ones… 'Special pills,' she says. She knows where he is right now and who he's with." Maureen glanced over at Sandra and shrugged. "Wow." She looked back down at the cell phone again. "She called me a bitcoin." Maureen didn't laugh. "Then she says, 'But I changed my mind so don't take one of those pills. If it works when you're with her, that'll absolutely kill me even though I don't want you anymore. And I won't want you. Not ever. I don't ever, ever want you near me again.' And then she says, 'In fact, don't bother to come home for your shift…'" Maureen laughed.

"I'm going to hire somebody to put all your shift in your stupid truck and you can just duck off forever. I'm changing the locks.'"

Mouth slightly agape, Maureen flipped her purse open and set the cell phone down inside it. "I probably didn't kill him. I'm probably off the hook."

Sandra looked over at her friend, first with compassion, then with alarm. "Maureen?"

"What?"

"Did you hear that?"

Male voices came from the other side of the wooden door.

"They must of gone in here. The tape's off."

"I'm not going in there."

"Why not. It's just… just… They're just symbols. You don't believe in any of that mumbo jumbo, do you? I know you're like, uh… you're… you're…"

"I think 'black' is the word you're searching your tiny little brain for, Brian?"

"Uh. Yeah. Black. I know you're black and everything, but you don't believe in any of that. Do you?"

"What if I dooooo believe in voooooodooooo?" Fake evil laughter followed his comment.

"Fuck off."

Sandra made a quick move to Muffy's lap to switch off the powerful flashlight sitting there.

Darkness. The darkest of darknesses.

"Not every black person is into voodoo, you know. I'm a fucking Lutheran. Like my parents. And grandparents."

"I still say you can fuck off with all that."

A scrape of wooden door on rock.

Then a presence beside them. The whispering voice of the presence was husky, muffled and male, and from the angle it came down to them, it indicated that the man was very tall.

"Come with me." An almost undetectable pin-light showed an opening in the tunnel's rock wall. The pin-light bobbled as the wheelchair moved through the opening. Sandra and Maureen followed.

From the area near the wooden door, a light shot past them, down the tunnel. The pin-light went out. A panel slid without the slightest sound across the opening, putting them in the darkest of darknesses again.

"Who are you?"

"Shh."

6

THE THINNEST SLIT of flickering light showed around the edges of the panel as the workers approached. It did nothing to brighten the space Maureen and Sandra were in with this strange man who, it seemed, had just rescued them from discovery.

"Shh."

"Hey, Brian. Did you hear about the dude that disappeared down here a few years ago?"

"Yeah, and that's pure bullshit."

"What if I told you it wasn't bullshit? They never found him, y'know. They're still looking."

"Yeah. I'm sure they are. They care so much about losers who go missing."

The sound of their voices indicated that Brian had stopped right in front of the panel and the other man had gone further down the tunnel.

"Oh oh, Brian. You're not going to like this."

"What?"

"It's a dead end. Come here."

"I believe you."

"Yeah right. Come here. *They* aren't going to believe me. I need you to back me up."

"You remind me about that loser getting lost down here in this voodoo cave we're in and you're telling me bullshit about a dead end? No frickin' way, man."

"Never mind. I'll take a picture of it with my cell. Won't prove a damn thing except that you're an asshole."

"All right, all right."

The thin slivers of light around the panel disappeared putting the hiding space in complete darkness again.

From down the corridor, "No shit? It *is* a dead end. Sorry there, buddy. This makes it even creepier, doesn't it?"

"Speak for yourself. Doesn't scare me a bit. Just makes me wonder how that dude could possibly have disappeared from someplace that doesn't have an exit." A pause. "Or would that be an entrance?" The evil laugh again.

"Fuck off."

Laughter erupted from "Buddy" as the light strips around the panel's perimeter appeared again then disappeared. "Guess that homeless guy was bullshitting about the women falling down here." More laughter. "Or maybe they *just disappeared*, too, eh?"

"Fuck off."

Sounds of scraping and banging from the area of the big wooden door meant the men were leaving.

Inside the space, the pin-light came on again. The panel slid away and the man helped the women exit with the wheelchair.

His presence and his pin-light evaporated into the space and the panel slid shut.

Fumbling, Maureen reached for the flashlight between Muffy's legs. The light filled the tunnel. "Oh my God, that was something, wasn't it?"

"Where did he go? And who was he?"

"I dunno. He sounded funny, too. Was he maybe wearing a mask or something? Weird."

"Don't go doubting yourself now, Maureen. Aren't you the one with that sixth sense or whatever you call it? How come you didn't predict that guy showing up?" Sandra didn't laugh.

Once again, men's voices drifted through the wooden door.

"Do you think we need all three boards?"

Laughter from Buddy. Then, "It's the only way to be sure." More laughter from Buddy.

Maureen and Sandra covered their mouths to stifle their giggles.

Sandra said, "That's a line from Aliens, isn't it?"

Maureen could barely control her laughter. "Yeah. The other guy didn't get it."

"But… Boards can only mean one thing."

The sounds of hammering bounced off the walls of the tunnel.

"We've gotta get out of here," said Maureen.

"Well… If they're nailing the door shut and there's a dead end around the corner, it looks like you're not going to jail for murder after all. Face it. We're going to die in here."

Maureen had just dumped the contents of her purse onto the tunnel floor. "It's gone. His phone is gone. I put it just inside my purse. On top of everything. It's gone."

Sandra picked up the big flashlight from between Muffy's legs and, grimacing, felt around between his thighs and under his scrotum. "It's not here. Are you sure you put it in there?"

"He took it. That guy took it. What are we going to do? And I didn't murder anybody. His wife did. He's not dead anyway. At least I don't think so."

"Looks like you got what you wanted but not in the way you expected." Sandra shone the flashlight around on the floor, walls and ceiling before putting it back between Muffy's legs.

"What are you talking about?"

"You wanted to get screwed and you did."

"That doesn't even begin to get funny."

"So, She Who Can Predict Things, where do we go from here?"

Securing her umbrella-cane in her right hand, and grabbing a second flashlight from one of the pockets in the wheelchair, Maureen headed down the tunnel and around the corner.

The flashlight came on and Maureen called back to Sandra, "We're OK. It's not a dead end. What were they talking about? Come on."

Sandra knelt to put everything from Maureen's purse back into it. She hung the purse back around Muffy's neck, grabbed the handles of the wheelchair and followed Maureen's voice.

It was true. There was no dead end. Slanting downward slightly, the tunnel continued to its next curve.

"This reminds me of something," said Sandra, taking the second flashlight from Maureen and tucking it back into one of the wheelchair's pockets. "Oh yeah. Now I remember. Did you ever see that episode of Star Trek about the Horta?"

"I'm not sure."

"They go to this planet where some guys are mining stuff. Way down into the depths of it. And there's this big rock that comes out of the wall and burns the guys. But then Spock does his mind-meld thing with it and it tells him about its eggs."

"Oh, wait. That's the one where Spock is crying and everything? And he keeps saying, 'The children. The children.'"

"That's the one."

"Every time I see that one, I cry along with him."

"So I guess if we're nice to the Horta, it won't hurt us. And maybe it'll even kill the giant spider."

"Did anybody ever tell you you're mean as fuck?"

"Only you, my dear friend. Only you."

"I wonder where this leads to."

"Out, I hope."

7

THEY HAD GONE no further than perhaps twenty-five yards when a man's voice called out behind them. "Please to be haltink in trecks."

"What?" Maureen whirled around, losing her balance as she did so and dropping her umbrella-cane.

Beside her, Sandra let go of the wheelchair and reached out to prevent her friend from falling.

An elderly man in suit and tie stood there pointing a large pistol at the tunnel floor. "Please be takink steps toward openink in vall of tunnel. Go. Now. Or I be shootink you."

The women turned slightly to see that there was, indeed, an opening into the tunnel wall that had not been there. At least, they hadn't noticed it.

"Another hole in the wall?" said Maureen.

"Seems the City of Ottawa has the pox."

"What?"

"Pox. You know. Holes? The plague?"

"What?"

"Sorry. Lame joke. It actually doesn't make sense to me either. Sorry. Just trying to lighten things—"

"Please do not be talkink. Please do as I say. Enter. Now."

Sandra's free hand had barely touched the closest handle of the wheelchair when the man said, "No. Do not touch veelchair."

"Listen, mister." That hand went to her hip. "Or sir. Or whatever you are, why should we?"

"Yeah," said Maureen. "You're not the boss of us. Why the hell should we?"

The man raised his pistol to point it at her. "This why." He stepped forward between the wheelchair and Maureen and Sandra. "Now. Enter."

Maureen and Sandra exchanged glances, shrugged shoulders and did as they were told.

The man reached up with his free hand and touched something on the wall near the top of the opening. Just as the panel in the previous opening in the wall had done when the other man had hidden them from the workers, the panel quietly slid closed. This time, to block only the women inside.

"Hey, wait. Give me my purse."

It was too late. The panel had found its edge and Maureen and Sandra were once more in the darkest of darknesses.

"What the hell's going on?" asked Maureen.

"You're asking me? How would I know?"

"Hey. What's that?"

On the floor, all around its circular edge, a thin bead of almost florescent light shimmered. Although the light was strong, it did nothing to brighten the space.

Sandra raised her head to look at the ceiling. "Same thing up there, too. What are we in?"

"You're the construction expert."

"It's like we're in some kind of tube. Interesting."

"Sandra! We're in a hole in the wall with what's probably radioactive something-or-other and we were put here by some guy with a Russian accent and all you can say is, 'Interesting'?"

"Now you're getting into my realm. You ever watch that show, Mysteries of the Abandoned?"

"Can't say I have," snapped Maureen. "Sorry. I get cranky when I'm scared. Is that the one where they investigate hauntings? I'm not into that. At all. Maybe this is a test tube."

"No, no. Not that one. In this one they find all these abandoned buildings and tunnels and things. Some of them were built by the Nazis. Oh. Did you feel that?"

"Feel what?"

"I thought I, uh… Never mind. Anyway. The Soviets built some of those weird buildings, too. Or so they say. The good old Cold War, eh? Sometimes they find places that go back hundreds of years, though. It's cool. Some of the places they go into are really dangerous and go far, far underground. You should watch it some time."

"Do you think that guy is one of them? I mean, he's old enough."

"Nah. He's not much older than we are. If he even is."

"Maybe they left him in here to guard their secrets. Maybe he's even a ghost. And he's got a Russian accent. Oh no. And that gun of his looked authentic. Oh no." Maureen laughed. "I'm just teasing you. I can't believe you're actually into all that supernatural shit. At least all those cop shows I watch are real."

"It's not supernatural… *shift*. Those places are real, too."

"Next thing I know, you're going to be talking about giant spiders again. Wasn't it radioactivity that mutated those things?"

"More or less and I thought you didn't want us talking about spiders."

Maureen said nothing.

"By the way, did you know that the Soviets weren't the only ones guilty of playing around with radiation and things like that?"

"I'm changing the subject! How's this? Did you hear that?"

Sandra's gasp filled the darkness. "What? Wait. No. I didn't hear anything. What are you talking about?"

"I didn't actually hear anything. I'm changing the subject. Like this. I said, 'Did you hear that?' and I meant there's nothing to hear. I don't think there's anything creepier than no sound. I wonder how deaf people manage. Oh. I felt that, though."

"Me, too. Like a jiggle or something. And it's not making me feel any better. Are we moving?"

"I don't know. Were we before?"

"Let's keep the subject changed, OK, Maureen? We were talking about sound. Right? Being deaf? How's this? Do spiders' feet make a sound when they walk?"

"All right. You win. No more spider talk from me either. How did we get going on that anyway? Let's talk about getting sent to jail for murder. Or dying of starvation and dehydration in here where we can't see a thing. First one to die gets to be eaten by the one who lives."

Sandra laughed. "That wouldn't be so bad."

"Oh stop. I'm talking about cannibalism and you're…" Maureen laughed, too. "Now that was funny. Naughty, but funny."

"All right. I'll go along with you. Eh? What's that you say, dearie?"

"You're just full of inappropriate jokes today, aren't you?"

"Don't laugh, but—"

"If you notice, I'm not."

"Don't laugh, but I do have an appointment next week to have my hearing tested. It's going on me."

"Oh, Sandra. Sorry. That sucks."

"Could be worse. I could have to carry around one of those big horn things like they did in the old days." Sandra's laugh was cut short. "Hey, look. Those funny lights went out."

"Did you feel that?"

"I did."

"It's like a downward pressure or something. Or an upward pressure? Whatever. Very slight but—"

Soundlessly, the panel slid open again, and the silhouette of the elderly man with the Russian accent stood there, gun in one hand and an extremely bright flashlight in the other.

Maureen and Sandra shielded their eyes with their hands.

"Please to be exitink now, ladies. I brought umbrella for limpink lady."

With the gun hand, he pointed to the wall where Maureen's umbrella-cane now rested.

"Take it," he said without emotion.

Maureen settled her umbrella-cane in her right hand and waited for further instructions.

8

THE MAN TOUCHED the wall and the panel slid closed behind them. "You vill not make any attempt at escape. Unterstoot?"

"Unterstoot," answered Maureen.

"Stop," whispered Sandra.

"Why should I? I don't have to be polite to someone who's holding me prisoner, do I?"

"Might be good practice for you for when the cops find out you murdered that guy."

"I didn't murder him. His wife did. Remember?"

"Ladies. I standink right here in front of you. I hearink your vords. I feelink question, too, so I answer question. I sent by Xavier..." He pronounced it ZAY-vier. "... to save... how you say?... ladies' asses from possible death." He bowed slightly, turned away and beckoned from over his shoulder. "Please to be followink me."

They followed.

"Well, thank you," said Maureen. "What kind of death, might I ask?" Then she whispered to Sandra. "Didn't Hitler wave like that? Maybe he's not Russian. Maybe that's Hitler."

"When you end up in prison for real," whispered Sandra, "that attitude is going to get you put in solitary."

"Unlike you, Miz Sandra," said the man, "I havink no problems with hearink." He motioned with his hand again, indicating they face the tunnel wall.

"How did he know…?"

"Is this where we get shot?"

"Shh," Sandra warned.

The man stepped forward and tapped the rock wall four times. The rock wall opened. "Come. Come."

Maureen and Sandra stepped through and the panel slid closed behind them. Overhead lights flickered on to reveal another cylindrical tunnel. A short one.

"Peachy," said Maureen.

"Ve have canned peaches," said the man as he turned off his flashlight. "But if wish to have real peaches, I vill try arrange for you."

"I didn't mean real peaches. It's an expression."

"I was makink joke," said the man.

"Two of them now with their lame jokes. Spare me, Lord."

"I heard that."

"Your friend not beink so deaf after all. Da?"

They had arrived at a huge metal door, perhaps thirty feet high and nearly as wide. The man went to the side and huddling over, appeared to tap a section of the wall with his finger several times. A small doorway within the larger door opened.

"We have arrived at next step." He bowed slightly and with a sweep of his arm, bade the women to pass through.

The rock-walled cavern they had just entered was every bit as large as the main door they had passed through. It was like being inside a huge snow globe, but without the fake snow.

"Come. Come." The man stepped toward the left and as he approached a spot on the floor that had a small X on it, the rock wall there slid sideways, leaving an opening into yet another tunnel. "Almost at final destination. Come. Come."

"Final?" whispered Maureen to Sandra. "I don't like the sound of that."

"Shh," said Sandra.

"No need for shh. All safe here. Very safe. Perfectly safe."

"Sorry, but I don't find that reassuring."

9

RISING FROM THE floor along the back and the right-hand side of the next chamber they stepped into were several high office partitions, translucent, but painted with delicate pale green and yellow leaves that entwined among each other. The floor was flat and tiled in an intricate and appealing pattern of white and pale yellow. The open space in the center of the chamber appeared to be a mishmash of living room, dining room, entertainment room, exercise room and possible office. On the left wall were several actual doors. These were closed. On the smooth stone wall beside the doors' jams were symbols, indecipherable at this distance.

"I'm in here, Doctor Molotov." A somewhat familiar but unmuffled male voice seemed to echo off the stone wall behind the partitions on the right.

"That's you?" asked Maureen. "You're a doctor?"

"It is. I am. Go."

Doctor Molotov prodded Maureen and Sandra to pass between two of the partitions. Maze-like, across from this entrance, a wide partition ran several feet in both directions, creating a corridor to both the left and the right.

Doctor Molotov urged them to turn left. This corridor led into a wide space surrounded by more partitions.

"Scary and comforting at the same time," said Maureen, glancing around.

Sandra took hold of Maureen's upper arm. "No. This is totally freaky."

Another opening showed what could only be an office space. Doctor Molotov pushed them toward it, then into it.

The back wall was rock. From here and there, tiny waterfalls flowed into the same long, narrow pool at the bottom of the wall. It was filled with plants whose leaves were pale green and yellow and intertwined with each other like the paintings on the translucent partition walls. A man on one knee by the pool, and with his back to them, appeared to be tending to something.

Sandra was the first to speak. "Beautiful."

"But what are they? I've never seen anything like them."

"They're obviously aquatic, but that's about all I can say except, gorgeous."

Doctor Molotov spoke. "Ladies? May I introduce my good friend Xavier? Xavier, please make the acquaintance, in person, of Maureen and Sandra."

The man tending to the plants was just now rising to his full height: about six and a half feet. His back was to them. He was skinny. On his head was a black stovepipe hat with feathers sticking out from it which made him appear to be even taller.

Xavier turned.

Both women screamed.

"For the love of God, Xavier. Do you have to do that every time you meet someone new?"

Xavier, a black man, was in full Vodou-Master regalia including a painted white face with black around the eyes. In a thick Haitian accent, he spoke: "Do like me say, *mesdames*, an' I won't hab to lay curse upon you."

Doctor Molotov managed to stop Maureen from running out of the room but he wasn't as lucky with catching Sandra.

"Xavier. Stop it. And do not! Do not do your evil laugh. You're going to give these old dolls a heart attack." He helped Maureen sit on a green, leather-covered bench that sat against one of the partitions. "I'll be right back." He rushed away.

Maureen's makeshift cane slid to the floor.

Xavier approached her. "I thought you didn't believe in this shit." His Haitian accent had disappeared. He grasped her elbow to help her stand.

"I don't. And what are you doing?"

He turned her to face away from him. "I'm fixing your hip."

"And just how do you expect to do—"

Xavier threw his right arm around against the top of Maureen's chest, just at collar-bone level. He pulled back and drove his hip into hers in one motion.

"There," he said. "All better. Now excuse me. I'll go wash my face."

He stepped behind another partition, this one clouded with dozens and dozens of leaves. Water splashed. A moment passed. Then the elderly and very handsome Xavier stepped out.

"Try to walk," he told Maureen who was standing there with her mouth looking like that of a cat who had just sniffed something stinky.

She seemed to recover. "Ah. Yes. Of course. Would you please hand me my cane then? I dropped it." She pointed to her umbrella on the floor.

"You don't need it anymore."

"I happen to have a dislocated hip. I can't walk without support."

"Try it." Xavier moved closer to her. "I'm here. I'll catch you if you fall. But you aren't going to."

Maureen looked up into his eyes. She took a step. "No shit! Sorry, 'scuse my Fr—" She laughed. "My English."

"Now walk to the wall and back."

At first with cautious steps, Maureen walked toward the wall. Halfway there, she picked up speed. On the way back, she was close to dancing. "This is amazing. What did you do to fix my hip?"

Xavier's eyes sparkled. Again in the Haitian accent, "I curse you. Remembah?"

Maureen giggled and flapped one hand at him. "Oh stop." Pink filled her cheeks. "Who are you? I mean really who are you? And why are you all dressed up like some voodoo witch doctor?"

"Maybe because I *am* some Vodou witch doctor?"

"You're hilarious. I like you."

Their conversation was interrupted by Sandra's squeals of complaint. She was being guided back into the room by Doctor Molotov. "Get your hands off me! How dare you!"

"Please be seated," said Xavier. "And don't run off again, Sandra. You have no idea what's out there." A fake evil laugh seemed to come all the way from his toes.

Doctor Molotov rolled his eyes.

The women sat immediately.

Sandra whispered to Maureen. "Is he for real?"

"No. He's just joking," Maureen said.

"I can assure you, ladies," said Doctor Molotov. "He's not joking. Not at all. He is for real."

Two beeps from Xavier's pocket caused him to place a finger in his ear and turn away. "Excuse me. *Bonjou.*"

"Wait a minute," said Maureen to Doctor Molotov. "Where did your accent go?"

"What accent? I don't have an accent. Well, aside from my Ottawa Valley accent which is the same as yours so that's why I can say I don't have one but other than that I—"

In the background, Xavier was talking in brief spurts. "Yes. Yes. She'll be glad you found it, Rocky. Great. Superb. Thank you."

Doctor Molotov said, "I use that accent on those who come here without an invitation. It instills fear, therefore obedience." He forced a smile at them.

Sandra's eyes were darting from Xavier to Maureen to Doctor Molotov to Xavier to Maureen. "Who are these people?"

"And it worked, didn't it?" laughed Doctor Molotov.

Maureen and Sandra exchanged rolled eyes and shrugs.

Xavier approached them again. "Sorry about that." He smiled. "Your phone has been found. Where were we? Ah, yes." He motioned with his hand to Doctor Molotov. "Stand by the doorway in case one of them tries to bolt again. We can't have that, can we?"

"That's the last thing we want to happen. Because it might actually *be* the last thing that happens. To *them*."

"Are you guys making fun of us?"

"We're trying to save your lives." Xavier pulled a chair close to the bench the women were sitting on and he sat on it, elbows on knees and leaning forward. "All righty. Who is going to be the one to spill the beans?"

Both Maureen and Sandra crossed their arms and sat back.

"Very well then." He turned to Doctor Molotov. "You take Sandra and I will question Maureen."

"You want me to do the questioning? Or Doctor Koi?"

Xavier turned to Maureen and Sandra. "Are you two gals an item? I mean are you partners? Wives of each other or anything like that?"

"Hell, no!" said Maureen. "What do you think I am?"

"Nice. Nice," said Sandra. "I'm your best friend and you think I'm some kind of monster that you wouldn't be caught dead being? I'm two-spirited. A Lesbian. So what. Big deal. I'm proud of it. You should be proud that I allow you to be my friend."

Maureen's face was not the cute pink shade it had been earlier when Xavier had made her blush. No. It was glowing bright red.

"Doctor Koi…" said Xavier with a big wide grin, "… may use any tactics called for during the questioning."

Doctor Molotov turned away and made his Hitler wave from behind his head again. "Let's go, Sandra."

"What the hell are you guys talking about?" demanded Maureen as Sandra rose to follow Doctor Molotov.

"Relax, Grasshopper. You'll find out soon enough."

10

MAUREEN WAS ONCE again alone with Xavier whose facial expression had become serious enough to make her lean away from him with her fingers poised to plug into her ears.

With loose hands, he grasped her wrists to lower her arms. "I'm not going to hurt you. Not with my words or with anything else. I merely need answers. All right?"

With her eyes watching him sideways, Maureen bowed her head.

"I need to know what you ladies are doing here. I need to know the truth. The absolute one-hundred-percent truth. If you tell me, then maybe—just maybe—I'll let you know why this is so important." He pulled open a door in the side table beside the bench. It was a storage-cabinet-refrigerator combo. "Lives are at stake."

From the tiny cabinet-refrigerator, he extracted a bottle of water that he handed to Maureen. After moving a small table in beside her at the bench, he placed a tray of biscuits and cheese on it.

Maureen muttered a thank you but touched nothing.

"That's perfectly safe, you know. See?" He made a sandwich with a piece of cheese between two biscuits and bit into it. "See? No frothing at the mouth." He set it down and leaned forward on his knees. "Main thing I need to know is, from whom did you get the powder?"

"Powder?"

"Your boyfriend—the one in the wheelchair—was dosed with something that only a *bokor* would know how to make. Or a *caplata*, perhaps? Who gave you the powder?"

"I have no clue what you're talking about. And he's not my boyfriend."

"You gave him something."

Maureen sighed.

"I know you gave him something. We heard you and Sandra talking."

"That's impossible."

"What's impossible? That you gave him something? Or that we can hear everything that goes on in the lava tubes?"

"The whats?"

"The tunnels. What's impossible?"

"Both."

"Don't lie to me."

"I gave him a Viagra."

Xavier laughed. "I know. And it was so very far past its best-by date, giving him a piece of celery would have affected him more. I'm talking about the powder. Where did you get the powder?"

"I'm sorry. I know nothing about powder. I know about his wife switching pills on him. She said she got something from somebody so she could make fake Viagra pills but—" Maureen frowned. "Or did she say the guy made the fake pills? Yeah. I think that was it. There's a text on Muffy's cell phone from her. You guys took his phone. You don't have to ask me. Find out for yourself. I forget."

"So you know this woman."

"I didn't even know the asshole had a wife in the first place so how would I know her?"

"She called you a bitcoin. Autocorrect for bitch. Between women that usually indicates they know each other."

"I have no idea who she is no matter what she says. And anyway, what are you saying? What powder? I'm a nurse, I can probably understand what you're talking about."

"Have you ever heard of frog powder? Or zombie powder?"

Maureen laughed. "Of course. In movies. Jeepers. We're the same age. You must have seen all those great fifties and sixties movies in the old days, too."

"In the old days, they didn't let us black folks into those white-man's movie theaters. Remember that?"

"Huh? What? Really? I… I thought everything changed for you guys after the Civil War. When was that? Uh. 1864?"

"What planet are you from?"

"Earth, assho—! Uh. Sorry. I grew up in a small town up the Valley. Everybody was either English, Irish, French or Polish. Catholic or Protestant was the real biggie. Oh, there were Indigenous people lived there, too, but they just kind of blended in with the French guys. Mostly for safety's sake. There was one Chinese family who had a restaurant. I don't think I ever saw a single one of them. Our family didn't do take-out in those days. How about yours? Did th…?"

Xavier's expression made Maureen apologize and go back to the subject.

"No black people, though. But I'm sure if there were some black kids around, they would have let them go to the Saturday afternoon matinees."

"My apologies for assuming. I'm overly sensitive, I guess. Years of programming. Sorry for the diversion. Now. Back to the question. Who gave you that powder? I need to know."

"Why?"

"Why what?"

"Why is it so important that you find out?"

"Guess who's going to get blamed for it if the police find out somebody's going around turning straying husbands into zombies."

"WHAT?"

"Ah. You *don't* know."

"Fuck, no. Oops, sorry. *Flip*, no. Far as I know, it was her. You have his phone. I told you. Go get it and read her text."

"I've read it. I had to make sure you weren't involved at least with the powder. So now that we've got that out of the way, why are you here?"

"I… I guess I might as well tell you the whole truth, eh?"

"You might as well." He pushed the plate of cheese and biscuits closer to her, but she still touched nothing. "And by the way, we returned all the items you stole from the construction site."

"Borrowed. The word is borrowed." She placed her bottle of water down. "You're not like… like an undercover cop or anything, are you?"

"If I were, telling you would pretty much defeat the purpose of my being one, wouldn't it?"

Maureen laughed. "I do like you. You are funny."

"Why are you here?"

"I'm here because I thought I killed that Muffy guy. And I asked my friend Sandra to help me bury him at the construction site because she used to work construction and knows how to run those digger things and stuff like that but when we were standing there, because of all the rain, the ground slid out and we ended up down at the bottom of their basement or whatever they call it and then we heard somebody coming and I was afraid—"

"OK. OK," said Xavier, patting her knee. "I got it. You're here because of Karma."

She laughed again, "That's what that homeless guy, Jerome, told the cop."

"His name's Rocky."

"You know that cop?"

"No. Jerome. Jerome's name is Rocky. And he's not homeless, he's one of us." Xavier grinned. "One of us, one of us."

"One of us?"

Xavier tried to suppress a smile, but he didn't do it well. "I may not have been able to see that many movies as a kid, but they play all the old ones on TV around Halloween. I watch *that* one every year. You've never seen that one? 'One. Of. Us. One. Of. Us. One. Of. Us.' You don't remember? It was called Freaks. It came out in the early 1930s."

"Hey! Come on. I'm not *that* old!"

"Neither am I, dear girl." He stood up and reached out his hand toward her. "Let's go. I have something to show you."

Maureen declined his outstretched hand and stood on her own.

"Very well." Xavier opened the door to the cabinet-refrigerator and slipped the plate and the water inside then strode toward the opening between the partitions.

Maureen adjusted her hippy-duds dress then looking up, realized that Xavier had paused at the opening and was standing there looking at her with an approving smile on his face.

Her cheeks flushed. "Oh stop."

"I don't think I deleted that movie," he said, taking her hand. "I probably still have it. We can watch it together. In the dark. Tonight. And when you get scared, I can protect you. Maybe you'll thank me by letting me seduce you. How about that?"

"And maybe I lied and I have some of that powder in my pocket and will slip it into your drink when you're not looking. Nobody's going to be doing any seducing around me."

"Good to hear," laughed Xavier. "Let's go."

11

NOW IN THE main hall, Xavier led Maureen to the opposite wall. As they passed by the doors cut into the rock of that wall, she noticed that painted near the first one was a starfish, on the second one, a volcano, and on the third, a small pebble.

Pointing, she asked, "What do these symbols mean?"

Xavier did not reply.

The picture on the door Xavier had brought Maureen to was a smiley face. A smiling one. Not the big-grin smiley face, but the plain, calm, gently smiling one. The next door had two smiley faces. He tapped the wall three times with his index finger and the door slid open with a *Star Trek*'s *Enterprise* squeak.

"See?" He pulled her toward the jam on his side and pointed. "See that spot there? The faint yellow rectangle on the rock? If you come closer, you can see twelve white squares."

Maureen leaned in to see where he was pointing. "Like on a phone."

"Exactly. Tap in your code and bingo, more curses are fulfilled. Your door opens."

"But how does it work? That's, like, rock! A special kind of paint or something?"

"Nope. Not painted. You'd have to take that up with the scientists. I'm just an MD. Your code is 666."

"Really. Seriously. Are you aware what those numbers stand for?"

"They stand for a subconscious warning—on top of all the other warnings you're going to be hearing during your stay—that danger lurks almost everywhere." He let go of her hand. "I'll show you around." He stepped inside.

"Wait. You said, 'during my stay.' What… uh… What exactly do you mean by *that*?"

"Exactly what it sounds like. Now, here is your apartment. What do you think of it? It's just the basics but who needs more than the basics?"

The room—or "apartment," as Xavier had called it—was sphere-like with smooth walls and ceiling. The light from the still-open door gleamed in a path across a flat, rock floor. At the far side, a wide swath of dark-brown, closed draperies hung from about halfway up the wall. To the right was a bar with three stools and behind it, cabinet doors and a shelf with what looked to be a small refrigerator and a microwave on it. Two doors at the far-right corner were closed. One of them had a wooden bar across it that sat in metal holders. Anything in the far-left corner was hidden from view by a partition much like the ones in the main hall, but opaque. Near the left was a sofa, two comfortable-looking stuffed chairs and a small television. From the wall near the TV hung a large box with wires leading out of it, reminding Maureen of her days in the ER, looking after those who usually ended up being terminal patients.

"Is this wallpaper?" Maureen reached out one hand to slide her fingers over the rounded wall just inside the entrance. "It's rock! How can it be so smooth?"

"Never heard of erosion?"

"Uh, yeah. But this is… uh…" Her eyes traveled all around the sphere, taking everything in. "This is…"

"All of the caves here have been eroded over millions of years. They've had extra help but… Well, I'm not the expert so that's about all I can say. If you want details, you need to ask Rocky."

Maureen chuckled. "So *Rock*y's a *rock* expert. Wait. Do you mean he's an actual geologist?"

"Yup."

"So that's what the little pebble symbol beside the other door means. That's his place."

Xavier nodded.

"And your name… Xavier. Is that supposed to be like 'Savior' or something? You're an actual medical doctor?"

Xavier tried to hide his growing smile but was having little success with that feat. He nodded.

"So is it possible then that this Doctor Koi you guys spoke of could have something to do with fish?"

"You got it." His laughter erupted in full force. "She's a marine biologist. You are one smart lady. I like you."

Maureen laughed along with him but not with nearly as much enthusiasm.

"Can you guess what Doctor Molotov's specialty is?"

"Explosives."

"Nope. Volcanologist."

"Now you're really freaking me out."

Xavier, grinning down at Maureen, sang, "*We've only just begun…*" He took her arm. "Let me show you where the alarms are."

12

"OK. OK," SAID Maureen, pulling herself away from Xavier's grasp. "That's it. I'm not going to look at anything else until you tell me what the fuck is going on here. What are all these alarms for? They're like every two feet!"

Xavier headed toward the seating area. "Every five feet. And they're not everywhere. Just... almost everywhere." He motioned for Maureen to follow him.

She did.

They sat.

Xavier sighed.

"Tell me."

"We are all in danger here. Everyone. All of us."

"In danger from what?"

Xavier paused. "There are natural enemies, of course. That's why we have all the alarms." His eyes met Maureen's. "Do you know how

Earth formed?"

"You mean, like, at the very beginning?" She shrugged. "Sandra's the one you should be asking. She into all that stuff."

"I'm no expert either," he said, face serious. "But 'according to my sources,' the crust cooled and became the surface. The molten stuff below came up through volcanoes that spewed up lava that formed mountains and valleys. Water in the valleys and in other low places became lakes and seas. The continents were formed. They split up. They stuck back together again. They split up. More seas. Some very deep seas. Some underground seas. There. Five billion years or so in a nutshell."

"That sounds familiar, yes, but what's that got to do with anything?"

"Life began. Life evolved. Intelligent life."

"So it did and that I know but what's that got to do with being in danger? Is there an earthquake coming or something? I know the Ottawa Valley's on a… a thingamabob. One of those uh, those—"

"Faults. They're called faults." Xavier rose to his feet. Holding his hand out to Maureen, he said, "Come with me. I'll show you." He led her to the door with the wooden bar across it then turned to face her, his face deadly serious once more. "You must always, always, always make certain that this door is blocked off at all times."

She shrugged. "OK."

"I'm serious. No matter what, this door must remain blocked." He lifted the wooden bar from its holders and set it on end beside the door. "Ready?"

She nodded.

Xavier pulled the door toward him to reveal a staircase that went up perhaps fifteen feet into a dark opening. On the back of the door was a huge bolt that would slide into the mechanism on the wall just inside the stairwell. The smell of seawater drifted down. "Up you go," he said.

"That's OK. I'll follow you. Go ahead."

As they climbed the staircase, Xavier spoke quietly. "We also block the door from this side when we leave our apartments. No matter the reason."

"Should I...?"

"I don't want you to feel trapped. You don't know me. We'll be just a moment, so we can leave it open this time. This time only! And try to keep your voice low. In fact, it's better if you don't speak at all." He stopped to turn back to Maureen with his now-familiar controlled grin. "Think you can manage that?"

"Oh stop."

Xavier paused at the top of the staircase to reach back for Maureen's hand. "Careful up here. The ledge is not very wide."

She took his hand and stepped up onto the landing.

The landing was about three feet square and from it ran a ledge of the same width all along the curving-inward rock face for about fifteen feet until it turned away to the left; it ran along the rock face behind her, too. At Maureen's left side was an opening in the rock, like a small cave. At the back of the small cave was a doorway into a cubicle.

"Yes. That's an elevator," said Xavier quietly. "Any time you hear the alarm, you must—and I cannot emphasize the word must enough, but you *must*—drop what you're doing no matter what it is—even if you are on the toilet—and run up here into that elevator. But bolt the door on the inside. The rest of us will be here within moments of your doing that and some of us might even beat you to the punch."

Maureen stared at him with a cat's stinky-face again.

"I'm sure you're familiar with the term 'certain death'?"

Maureen continued to stare at him, her eyes widening now, too.

"And yes, I do mean to scare you."

Maureen grabbed hold of Xavier's sleeve as she leaned toward the rim of the ledge. Even in the semi-darkness, the glitter of water was unmistakable. She whispered, "Water?"

Xavier nodded then pointed downward along the rock wall to a ledge below that ran about fifty feet. It was barely above water level. A patch of light on the ledge at the far end revealed two people sitting there as though enjoying a sip of wine on a patio.

"Is that Sandra?" Maureen smiled.

"She's with Doctor Koi."

Maureen called out, "Hey! Sandra. Up here."

Before she could even get her arm up to wave, brilliant neon-green light flooded the enormous, stomach-shaped cavern they were in. The light glowed from the lower edges, the shores, of the long body of water that stretched into the distance in both directions, narrowing into continuing tubes at both ends.

"Hush! Dammit." Xavier slapped his hand over her mouth.

On the patio below—just as the woman called Doctor Koi whirled around to look up at them—from the water, a boulder the size of a 1960's Volkswagen Beetle leaped out to land on top of Sandra.

Sandra screamed and her scream echoed, echoed, echoed.

Maureen's muffled scream from behind Xavier's hand melded with Sandra's echoes, echoes, echoes.

Doctor Koi screamed, "No, no, Don." Echo, echo, echo. "She wasn't doing anything. It's all right. It's all right. Get off her."

The boulder dissolved into the huge body and the eight flailing arms of an octopus as it slid off Sandra.

"Good boy. Good boy. Thank you."

The octopus stayed on the patio, moving three, then four of its arms several times before it curled all its arms around and under itself and settled.

"No need to apologize, Don. It's OK. She's not hurt. You're not hurt. Right, Sandra? You're OK?"

Eyes wide, Sandra's head bobbed up and down. She drew her knees up to her chest and hugged them.

The neon-green lights dimmed somewhat, but didn't go out entirely.

Maureen pulled herself away from Xavier's hand. "What in the name of fucking hell is that thing?"

The octopus's arms flailed again, and Doctor Koi muttered something to it.

"That 'thing' is why we're still alive down here."

"Is that where the danger you were talking about comes from?"

"Nope." Xavier pointed upwards with his left thumb and then with his eyes.

Maureen looked upward, too. "I don't see anything."

"I mean on the Surface. That's where the most danger will come from if the police think I'm the one turning people into zombies."

"Really. Oh."

He pointed down at the water. "From there, too, but that's only natural. Isn't it? We all have to eat, don't we?" Then his finger traveled from one end of the cavern to the other. "Plus, the lava tubes are everywhere and… Well. We don't need to go into all that right now, do we?"

With wide eyes, Maureen looked down over the side of the ledge. "Seriously? We're in danger of being eaten and you're saying that real life up there…" She pointed. "… is more dangerous? What could be worse than being eaten by an octopus?"

Xavier took her chin in hand so he could stare into her eyes. "I guess I'll have to tell you sooner or later."

Maureen pushed him away. "If you're planning to keep me imprisoned here, I would like to know at least one reason why. So get with it. What's going on?"

"We're nearly half a mile below the bottom of the Ottawa River and this inland sea goes down maybe two or three more miles. Here and there, that is. It also goes for miles and miles on either side. We haven't been able to figure that one out yet though. Nobody wants to… uh… go exploring. It's dangerous enough right here."

"This is absolutely ridiculous!" Maureen's laugh burst out of her. "How the hell did you manage to get me down here then, pray tell! Sandra and me. With a Beam-Me-Up-Fuckin'-Scotty?"

This made the octopus wave his arms in a pattern again. He raised one of his left arms and made a hook with the end of it pointing to his right. He stretched that arm out to point it at Maureen, then formed it into a hook again. He then seemed to point it at his undersides.

Xavier laughed. "Don just asked Doctor Koi a question about you."

"What?"

"He asked her, 'Who is that vent?'"

"I didn't hear it say anything."

"Hand signals, my dear lady. He's been teaching us hand signals so we can communicate."

"And what's a vent?"

"I think it means asshole."

"You are so full of shit, it's no wonder your eyes are brown." And with that, Maureen stomped away toward the staircase and her hurried footsteps told Xavier she was nearly at the bottom when the word "Houston" echoed up the staircase.

Maureen's startled voice followed it. "What the—? You are totally creepy, you know that? Always showing up out of mid-air. Or mid-shadow, I guess I should say. What do *you* want?"

Doctor Molotov's voice called out, "You up there, Xavier? Is everything in good order? The doors are all wide open down here, you know."

"Yeah. I know," Xavier called out. "Giving a quick guided tour. What's up?"

"There's been another one. Oh. There you are."

Xavier stepped off the bottom stair. "Girlfriend called it in?" He turned to close the door and place the bar back into its holders.

Doctor Molotov shook his head. "Not this time. He was all by himself. Rocky says the guy passed out on the O-Train."

"What in the name of God are you guys talking about?"

Xavier grasped Maureen's elbow. "That makes zombie number three that the police have now. Magic number three means serial killer to them. I'm in big trouble. We're in big trouble."

"But they don't *know* about Muffy." Maureen's eyes formed slits as she glared at Xavier, then Doctor Molotov, then Xavier again. "Right? You didn't tell them, did you? I bloody hope not!"

"No, we didn't tell them because they'd better *not* find out about Muffy. Since he's in my possession, as it were, I—"

Doctor Molotov's laughter stopped Xavier in mid-sentence.

Xavier shrugged and shook his head in a question.

"'Possession'?" said Doctor Molotov. "A rather poor choice of words given the opinion the cops have of you, oh Vodou Master. Don't you think?"

"Um. Under my control? And nobody's possessed!" There was no smile or even a hint of one on Xavier's face.

"That's worse."

Xavier placed thumb and fingers on his forehead. "Whatever. What I was trying to say is, if they find him anywhere near me, in zombie-mode, there isn't anything I can say to convince them I was not the one who did that to him. And to them." Xavier turned Maureen to face him full-on. "Do you understand now why I need you to tell me where you got the powder?"

"I don't have the powder. I never had the powder. It was her. The wife. The wife knows. Not me. For God's sake, stop accusing me of something I didn't do!"

"Now you know what it feels like."

"OK, you two," said Doctor Molotov. "Break it up. The question is, what are we going to do about it?"

"See if you can get hold of Rocky. We'll meet in Doctor Koi's apartment. Don's already there so we don't have to go hunting for him."

Maureen tapped Xavier on the arm. "I have no clue what's going on. All I know is, I don't want to be here. Give me my purse, my phone, my wheelchair, my friend—not necessarily in that order—and show me the way out. You can keep Muffy."

Doctor Molotov waved for silence with the hand not holding his phone to his ear.

Xavier whispered, "I think you might change your mind once you learn what's at stake."

13

DOCTOR KOI'S APARTMENT was set up in a similar fashion to Maureen's but with the draperies wide open to expose the patio and the water beyond it. There was no partition there. Instead, there was one where the TV area in Maureen's apartment was. With barely the tips of two of his arms on the edge of the patio, the octopus bobbed in the water, staring at Maureen with one eye and at Xavier with the other. A flicker of the tip of its right arm closest to the octopus's head caused Xavier to wave at him, nod and smile.

Doctor Molotov followed them in. "He's on his way."

"Anyone care for anything? Tea?" Doctor Koi, a stunningly beautiful Asian woman in her eighties, was moving folding chairs toward the patio, two under each arm.

"Hey. Let me do that," said Sandra, taking two of the chairs.

"If so," said Doctor Koi. "You know where everything is. Help yourselves."

She and Sandra set the chairs in as much of a circle as they could, given the narrow dimensions of the patio and the finger-like tips of the octopus's arms in their way. It appeared that the octopus would be included in the circle.

"Doctor Koi, this is Sandra's friend Maureen. Maureen, may I present Doctor Koi and her friend, student and teacher, Don."

The octopus's arms brought him out of the water onto the patio where he flailed them around.

"He's pleased to meet you," said Doctor Koi.

Maureen laughed. "You call him Don. Cute. Is that because we live in Little Italy?" No one responded. "You know. The capo duh capi or something like that?"

The octopus flailed his arms again and Doctor Koi said, "That would be *capo di tutti i capi* and no. It's short for Poseidon. Posei*don*."

"Oh. Sorry. I…"

At this, the octopus launched himself toward Maureen, stopping right in front of her and raising himself up to have his strange, horizontally slitted eyes on a level with hers. His eyes rolled inwards as one of his arms snaked around behind her, holding her in its grasp. With the tip of another arm, he touched her bottom lip. A third arm came upside down from his side to reach her upper lip. Then, with the tips of the arms at her mouth, he very, very gently separated her lips.

"Don't move," cautioned Xavier.

The octopus's head turned slowly and he opened the slit of one huge eyeball to peer into Maureen's mouth.

Then like a punctured air-mattress, he collapsed and scutter-rolled toward the patio. He turned, and making the hook signal again, he waved his arms around at Doctor Koi. One of the shapes he made with two of his arms was a heart. Then with one arm, he formed a smiling mouth below his eyes. Then a hook again.

"Is that what I think it is?" Maureen asked. "He made a heart and a mouth?"

"Apparently, the heart shape can mean different things depending on context," said Xavier.

"We're all learning from him," said Doctor Koi. "And I must say, he's very patient with us."

The octopus tapped Doctor Koi's shoulder and raised a hooked arm again.

"Most of the time," she smiled at the octopus, who laid an arm against his lower face in a smile again. "By the way, the raised hooked arm is a question mark."

Don raised the hooked arm.

"Yes. Like that."

"You talk to each other," said Maureen, stinky-faced cat again.

"They do," said Sandra, grinning widely. "Isn't that the coolest thing ever?"

"Um."

"And Don's hilarious. He's got the weirdest sense of humor."

The octopus tapped Doctor Koi again.

"Oh, sorry," she said. "I haven't answered Don's question yet." She turned to him. "Yes. It is."

More flailing and hooked question marks but this time, a faint green glow spread across part of what could be called Don's forehead.

"What did he say?" asked Maureen.

Doctor Koi was obviously trying to hold back laughter, but she managed to pat Don about where a human's cheek would be. "Do you want a direct quote?"

"Why not?"

"He said, 'I don't understand why you called her that before. She doesn't have any sugar in her mouth.'"

Maureen said "Tsk," but everyone laughed anyway.

Even Don placed two arms to form a laugh. Then he formed a heart that he aimed at Maureen.

A rumble. Felt, not heard.

"We were too loud," said Xavier.

Almost instantly, Don had turned a neutral bluish color and was instantly in the water, slapping it with one of his arms: one two three; with two arms, one two three; with one arm, one two three.

"Is that what I think it is?" called Doctor Koi.

Don raised the arm on his right closest to the center of his body upward.

"That's a yes," she said. "Evacuate! Now."

Behind her, Don continued to slap the water with his signals. Here and there, throughout the cavern, things moving under the water rippled the surface.

Everyone scrambled to get the chairs back inside the apartment. Doctor Koi rushed to one side of the draperies to tap something on the wall. A huge, darkened sheet of glass dropped down onto the patio floor without a sound. Xavier already had his hand on Maureen's elbow. Rocky, who had just that moment arrived, was halfway up the stairs and Doctor Molotov was setting the bar from the door aside. Doctor Koi had her arm around Sandra's back and was guiding her toward the stairs.

Almost blinding in its intensity, green-neon light filled the stairway as they ran upwards.

A slam and the sound of metal sliding into metal told them Doctor Molotov had waited below to bolt the door behind them.

In a chain of hands holding hands, Rocky, then Xavier and Maureen, Sandra and Doctor Koi, then Doctor Molotov, struggled along the narrow ridge toward the cave opening that Maureen and Xavier had just been at, and the elevator there.

"Don't look at the light," said Xavier. "Keep your eyes averted."

"What's doing that?" asked Maureen.

"Clusterwinks," said Doctor Koi.

"Yeah," laughed Maureen without humor. "Obviously it's some kind of clusterfuck. But I asked what's doing that?"

Doctor Koi said, "It's a clusterfuck of clusterwinks, sugarmouth. They react when frightened. It's coming."

Rocky, while twirling his long hair into a man-bun, guided everyone into the small, round elevator. Once they were all safely inside the elevator, he tapped the wall and the door slid shut. There was no familiar *Star Trek Enterprise*'s squeak. There was no sound at all except for the panicked breathing of the elevator's six occupants.

Maureen grabbed Doctor Koi's arm, and none too gently. "What's coming?"

"We don't exactly know what it is. Just that it's big, highly intelligent, and occasionally gets ravenously hungry."

14

A DIM LIGHT surrounding the elevator tube seeped in through minute cracks.

"What went on there?" asked Sandra. "What uh… What were those wild lights?"

"Clusterwinks," said Doctor Koi. "They're called clusterwinks."

Maureen giggled.

"It's not a euphemism, Maureen. They're snails. Like I said, they glow like that when frightened. Or to attract mates."

"The light is much brighter than it would normally be because of all the…" began Rocky. He looked up at Xavier who nodded approval. "Diamonds. The place is full of diamonds and diamond dust. And there are literally tons of weird metals and crystals down here that I can't even begin to identify. And most of them glow."

"This place overwhelms me more and more every day, too," said Doctor Koi. "I'd estimate that ninety-seven percent of the species I've come across so far should not be at this depth."

"Wow," said Sandra.

"It isn't even a 'depth' to start with. Some of the creatures I've seen here exist only four or five thousand meters below sea level at the most enormous pressures imaginable. But here they are. Almost at sea level. This sea level, I mean. I don't understand it. None of us does."

"The only thing I can come up with," said Doctor Molotov, "is that this sea—and it is a sea, right, Rocky? Doctor Koi?"

"It is," said Rocky.

Doctor Koi nodded.

"That this sea was somehow set apart and evolved separately. Must have happened during one of the continental collisions. Like at the time of Pangea maybe. Have you heard of that?"

Maureen frowned. "Pangea?"

"Turtle Island," said Sandra. "My wheelhouse."

"Oh. Right. Sorry. Of course. Please, Doctor Molotov, continue."

"You can call me Tovy if you like. Pretty much everybody else does."

The elevator shifted.

Sandra gasped. "Oh, no. What's happening now?"

Doctor Koi reached out to take Sandra's hand. "Nothing's wrong. We're OK. Some of the elevators don't go straight up in one shot."

Rocky said, "Or we'd have instability magnified to the hundredth power."

"Literally." Doctor Molotov elbowed Rocky. "Good one."

"Oh, right. Hah. I didn't intend the 'magnified' pun."

"You're getting as bad as Xavier with the Freudian slips."

Everyone laughed but Maureen and Sandra.

"I don't see anything funny about any of this," said Maureen.

"Neither do I," added Sandra.

"There, see?" said Doctor Koi. "We've stopped moving sideways and now we're going up again."

Xavier explained. "We go up about fifty stories' worth then sideways, then another fifty or sixty. It depends on... Well. It depends. On a lot of things."

"Oh really!" snapped Maureen. "Then how were Sandra and I able to get all the way down here in the first place without this going on? I think we would have noticed."

"We did," said Sandra. "Remember? A little jiggle here and there?"

"Oh. Right. Sorry. But how...? I mean, there's no sound. How can we be moving through rock with no sound?"

"That question," said Xavier, "you'd have to ask an engineer."

"OK. So which one of you is an engineer?"

Xavier, Doctor Molotov, Rocky and Doctor Koi exchanged grins.

"Don probably knows how it works," said Doctor Koi. "We haven't got a clue."

"Now *that* is funny," said Maureen.

She waited for a response.

None came.

"Isn't it?"

"He's really smart," said Sandra. "He really is."

"If he doesn't know, he would certainly find out for you if you asked him nice," said Doctor Koi. "He's got connections."

Maureen shook her head and muttered. "You guys are all nuts."

After a few more almost-imperceptible shifts, Rocky announced, "We made it. I'll go make sure the coast is clear." And off he went, leaving the rest of them waiting in the elevator tube.

15

WHEN ROCKY RETURNED with the all-clear, they stepped out into something like a locker room, but without lockers or showers. From there, they worked their way through a series of double-side-camouflaged panels, curving lava tubes, and short, manually chipped-out tunnels into an actual locker room, then through a normal doorway into a large space.

"A shelter?" whispered Maureen to Xavier who was leaning over her shoulder.

"More or less."

The room they were in was low ceilinged with cement-block walls that had been painted with cheerful images of action figures, angels, historical icons and animals and flowers, obviously created by different artists. Floor lamps with snaking cords plugged into power bars, some plugged into each other, gave the area an atmosphere of cheerful comfort. Halls led off here and there. The entire far corner was a cafeteria. Behind the counter, an elderly woman and man were shouting at each other as though they were in an episode of *Hell's Kitchen*. Three of the customer section's several tables had been moved close together, their chairs occupied by about a dozen seniors who seemed to be so engaged in conversation, they hadn't noticed their arrival.

"Are we invisible or something?" whispered Sandra.

Maureen whispered back. "Maybe having these guys just pop out of the walls is a regular occurrence."

"And that's supposed to make me feel better."

"You asked."

One of the men at the tables looked away from the group. "Hey, boss. We were just talking about you." He rose from his chair. He would be in his sixties and was in excellent physical shape. He crossed the room quickly, arms spread wide to embrace Xavier. Their hug was brief and without comment.

The man stepped away from Xavier and indicated Maureen and Sandra. "And these lovely ladies would be...?" His mouth smiled at them, but his eyes were doing inventory without moving from theirs.

"Maureen and Sandra. What's with the meeting? What's going on? Oh, this is Vainy."

"Hey!" said Vainy, his smile—such as it was—instantly disappearing. "Don't say it like that."

"Oh. Sorry. My Haitian accent must have slipped in. Ladies? This is *VAN*ni."

Vainy's such-as-it-was smile returned instantly and handshakes were exchanged. The inventory continued.

"Theo's missing," he said, making what looked like forced eye contact with Xavier. "They're all worried about him but personally, between you and I, he's around somewhere and up to no good. As usual."

"What? Theo's missing?" Xavier took three long strides toward the far wall but not before taking Maureen by the hand and dragging her along with him. "Meeting room. Right now," he called out. "Everybody."

"Yes, boss," said Vainy, his emotionless eyes now aimed at the group in the cafeteria, the forced smile still evident. "OK, everybody. You heard the boss. Let's go." He waved his arms and hands at them. "You heard him. Let's go."

"Boss?" said Maureen, almost running to keep up with Xavier. "He's calling you boss. You're their boss?" She reached behind her to take Sandra's hand and drag her along with them.

"I hire them for this and that sometimes. One reason is to give them a bit of an income. Homeless seniors don't do all that well on the streets. Helps with self-esteem. Main thing is, though, they have a lot to offer. A lot. Being homeless doesn't mean you are without talent or gifts. Most of the time, it's just the opposite."

"How come he went off on you like that?" asked Sandra.

Maureen added, "Yeah. Seemed a little over the top."

"Who? Vai—?" Xavier stopped walking and leaned down. He spoke quietly. "His name's Giovanni. Vanni for short. But we like to mispronounce it as Vainy. Behind his back, though. I slipped up."

Maureen shook her head. "I don't get it. Does he mainline drugs or something?"

"Not that kind of vein, v-A-i-n. You know. Like the song? You're So Vain? Carly Simon?"

"That's not nice."

"I used to berate everyone for doing that, but I don't anymore."

"Oh? Why is th—?

Sandra interrupted. "These guys are homeless? Wow. They don't look it, do they?"

"I'm homeless, too," said Xavier, holding the door to the meeting room open to allow Maureen and Sandra to enter. Behind him, Rocky grabbed the door from him. "Or I suppose I should say we are house-less. That would describe it better. Yes. Because we all have a home here."

A speaker's lectern faced several chairs set up in phalanxes. These were quickly being filled up by the men and women, all seniors, all healthy and spry, not a limp or a cane among them.

Behind the lectern were other chairs. Xavier led Maureen and Sandra to these. Rocky, Doctor Molotov and Doctor Koi—leaving one chair empty for Xavier—bookended them.

The last ones to enter the room were the pair from the kitchen, still squabbling but with quiet voices and hand signals, some rude.

"All right. So…" said Xavier from the speaker's lectern. "Looks like everybody is here.…" He seemed to do a head count. "Except for Theo, of course. Oh. Where's Pamela?"

"She went shopping," said Vainy from the outside chair in the front row.

"As if," said the Hell's Kitchen woman from the back of the room. "The last thing Pamela would do is go anywhere alone."

This made everyone hook their elbows over the backs of their chairs to turn around.

"Besides. We did that yesterday. Together. Barry, here, helped."

The Hell's Kitchen man beside her rose from his chair. He folded his hands together and said, "My name's Barry and I'm an alcoholic."

"Sit down," the woman said with kindness. "It's not that kind of meeting."

"Oh," said Barry. He partially sat then rose to full height again. "My name's Barry and I'm a drug addict."

"Barry," said Xavier with equally as much compassion as the Hell's Kitchen woman had used. "It's not that kind of meeting either."

Three women turned back to face the lectern again, two with adoring eyes on Xavier.

"We're here to see if we can find out where Theo went."

"I know where he went," said Barry. "But I can't tell anybody." His eyes went to Vainy and it was obvious that he hadn't meant that to happen. "Uh. I think so anyway. I *think* I know."

"Barry," said Vainy, rising from his chair. "You're getting mixed up again, aren't you? We always tell the truth here, right? There's nothing to be afraid of. What do you know exactly?"

"Maybe I don't know after all." Barry hung his head. "My name's Barry and…" The woman tugged gently on his arm and guided him down onto his chair. She whispered something that made him nod agreement.

That empty-eyed smile once again spread across Vainy's face as he turned forward toward the lectern. "You can tell me later, Barry. You know you can. I know you're afraid to say it out loud in front of everybody. But you can tell me. I am capable of keeping secrets."

Without making any unnecessary movements or sound, the rest of the group turned to face ahead, all eyes on the floor, even the eyes that had been adoring Xavier.

"Mostly everything that goes wrong around here is because somebody made it go wrong," said the woman. "I do not for one moment believe that Theo has taken off anywhere on his own accord without letting at least someone know. He's not like that. I think someone knows something and they aren't talking. And I don't mean Barry here."

"Hey, hey, now. Hey," said Xavier. "We're not here to throw accusations around. Don't go blaming Barry. We're here to see if we can find out where Theo is." He spread his arms out, palms up to encompass the group. "Isn't that right, everyone?"

Mumbles of agreement passed through the group.

"And Pamela too now it looks like," said the woman.

A mutter went through the group as frowning faces turned toward each other.

Xavier held his hand up. "Thank you, uh, Vanni. You maybe be seated. Thank you. Does anybody know anything? And I mean anything for sure, for sure?"

Another mutter went through the group. Shoulders shrugged. Vainy already had his cell phone out and was thumbing it.

"Well then. I guess the meeting is over." Xavier turned around to reach out for Maureen's hand. "Let's go check in on your boyfriend."

"Stop it. I told you. He's not my boyfriend." Ignoring Xavier's hand, she rose to her feet.

Sandra laughed. "See what you can get yourself into going on those dating sites?" She stood up, as did the others beside her.

Then someone from the phalanx of emptying, scraping chairs came forward. A man. He whispered, "I have something to say." He had a slight Haitian accent. He was dark-skinned like Xavier and tall and skinny like Xavier, too, with similar facial features and was probably around the same age.

Those who were still at the doorway stopped to turn. All eyes were on the man. Especially Vainy's.

He continued to whisper. "But I'm certainly not going to say it here where those who were once deaf can still read lips and even the walls have ears. Am I?"

Vainy strode from the room, knocking one of the elderly women against the doorframe as he passed her.

She opened her mouth to complain, but one of the other women and one man hushed her.

Xavier leaned toward the man. Quietly, he said, "The new guy's room. Now. The rest of you? Head up to street level. Have supper or something. Eyes and ears open and mouth shut. Right?"

Maureen stepped away to follow the others.

"Not you, though. You're not getting out of it that easy, dear girl. You're coming with us."

16

THE "NEW GUY'S room" was set up like a hospital room minus flowers and get-well cards. Every machine imaginable was beeping or showing squiggly lines or both. Lying there, quietly staring at the ceiling, was Muffy. The wires and tubes coming out of him made it look like he'd been caught in some giant spider's web. The barred sides of his bed were up.

The man immediately went to the head of Muffy's bed where he reached up to closely examine a feeding bag hanging there and, following the tubing down, he checked the intravenous port on Muffy's arm. He flipped up the sheet on that side then, without touching anything more, he leaned down to examine a tubed bag hanging off the side. He opened a drawer to remove a small bottle with a medicine dropper on it. With this, he put drops into Muffy's open eyes.

Xavier crossed the room to hover over Muffy. "Muffy, my good man. Feeling any different?"

No comment from Muffy.

Xavier turned to Maureen. "You try."

"Try what?"

A rustle of bedding made them glance at Muffy's face, but nothing had changed.

The man said, "Does he know you? It's like he recognized your voice or something. That's a good sign."

Xavier reached into a pocket at the foot of Muffy's bed and removed an iPad. He tapped it several times, then handed it to Maureen.

Maureen slid her fingers here and there on the iPad's screen with increasing speed. "What's this with the fentanyl overdose? He wasn't overdosed with fent—"

Xavier snatched the iPad from Maureen and said, "I forgot to introduce you to Stan here."

Stan touched his forehead with his index finger and smiled at her. His eyes were soft and kind. Then his eyes went to Xavier's but instead of the softness, there was a question in them.

"My apologies. I should have introduced you two right away. This is Maureen. Retired nurse. Retired ER nurse. Stan is a doctor but not a doctor for humans. He's a veterinarian."

"*Was* a veterinarian," said Stan with a slight smile. "Was. Many years ago. I never got to practice here. Not legally, at least."

"Where did you study?" she asked.

"Might as well have been Mars."

"Ah. Gotcha."

"And no amount of tests could prove my capabilities because of where I'd trained."

"His extensive capabilities," said Xavier, patting Stan's shoulder. "The science of medicine is essentially the same for all species, so we trust him here to tend to those who are dealing with drug overdoses, addictions and… and such."

Xavier and Stan exchanged glances.

"Why not?" continued Xavier. "He's very good at what we do here. Been doing it for a long time. Science is science. Right?" He slapped Stan's shoulder.

Maureen was barely listening. She was staring at Muffy. "So you think it was fentanyl she gave him and not that zombie powd—"

Xavier slapped his hand over Maureen's mouth. "Those words are not to be spoken here. Nobody knows about that. NOBODY!"

Stan reached out to pull Xavier's hand away from Maureen's face. "So I was right then. It's not fentanyl. It's something I don't want to think about." He stepped back from Xavier, the saddest of sad looks on his face. "Was it you? Why would you do that? We don't do that anymore. Ever. Not us. We're not controlled by the government anymore. We don't live there anymore. None of our family does either. We're safe."

Maureen wiped her mouth off. "Sheesh. You try that one more time and so help me…"

"I didn't," said Xavier. "I didn't. She…" His index finger pointed to Maureen. "She got…" He turned to her. "Sorry." Then back to Stan. "She got involved with this man…" He indicated Muffy, then his eyes flicked to Maureen's. "… somehow and… You wanna take this?"

"I met him on one of those online dating sites. His wife found out he was screwing around on her all the time and she found some guy who knows how to make fake Viagra pills. I guess she switched them out or something and he took one. I think. And I think maybe he gave himself a dose of nitroglycerin, too. I think. And we were having wine. And I…" Maureen's eyes looked like those of a puppy who had just been caught shredding a couch cushion. "And I ended up here. With Muffy. A dead Muffy. But Muffy wasn't dead. Xavier took over from there."

"Under any other circumstances that would be funny," said Stan. "But you lied to me, Xavier. When I'm looking after a patient, I need to know exactly what to treat him for. I can't be just… just willy-nilly giving him antidotes to what I *think* he has taken. Are you going to blame me when he dies? That is not fair, Xavier. Not fair whatsoever. The treatments I've been giving him since his arrival— Oh, man! We've done no research on— Oh, man! I—"

"There's something going on that you aren't aware of."

"Obviously! But you could have told me. You should have told me he'd been dosed. And here I was thinking somebody was sneaking in here and poisoning him with something. Maybe even Vainy. I'll have to apologize to him now. Thanks a *lot*."

"The fewer who know, the better."

"You don't trust me."

"I would trust you with my own life, but this is… This is different."

"Ahem."

All three whirled toward the door. It was Barry.

"Missus Cheffie wants you, Stan."

"What for?"

"I forget. But I think it will be OK if Xavier comes, too. Or maybe she didn't tell me so that means I didn't forget then. Right? Yeah. I think she didn't tell me. And that lady. I know her from somewhere. She can come, too. She's nice. Missus Cheffie freaked out when she— Oh. Now I remember. She found Theo."

"Excellent," said Xavier, heading toward the door.

Without being prompted, Maureen followed him.

"Do I need to bring anything?" asked Stan. "First aid kit or anything?"

Barry looked at the floor. "Probably not."

"Why," asked Stan. "He's OK, right?"

"Well. She kinda found him lying on the floor in the walk-in fridge, eh?"

17

IN THE WALK-IN fridge, Xavier and Stan were on their knees on either side of an elderly male.

"This tells me we can safely rule Theo out as the one I'm looking for," Xavier said to Maureen, who was across from him, standing over Stan.

"Think he was he dosed with something?" asked Stan. "You know. With that certain something you kept secret from me?"

Xavier looked up at Maureen. "No needle marks. At least, no new ones."

"You and I both know that doesn't go in with a needle. Is he even dead?" Stan tipped the man's body up sideways to raise his shirt far enough to examine his back. "No blood pooling. Good. And bad at the same time."

Xavier still did not reply to Stan.

"Does he have any girlfriends?" Maureen asked. "You know, that he might have, you know, used Viagra for and it got mixed up with something else?"

Stan sighed. "Not that I know of."

"Listen," said Xavier, rising to his feet. "We have to bring Officer Bob in on this."

"I agree," said Stan as he pulled a large kitchen towel up to Theo's chin before standing up.

"Muffy's wallet has his ID and address and everything in it?"

"Yes."

"I think you and Officer Bob need to find Missus Muffy."

"I think so, too."

"Or maybe send Rocky instead. I need you here and I'll be needing a report from Officer Bob. Rocky can do that. My crew has to be filled in on this. Dammit."

Stan nodded.

"Be sure Officer Bob knows that Muffy was administered the uh… the special substance."

"You're going to tell the cops about me and Muffy? You promised."

"I don't make promises, dear girl. I only demand that other people make them." His laugh was ignored. "But he won't know you're involved. Not yet. Officer Bob knows about the others. All of them. That's how we found out about the guy on the O-Train. Officer Bob knows everything that's going on in his hood. Always."

Xavier returned Maureen's frown.

"Oh. He's retired. He's not a cop anymore. He just runs 'Hood Watch now. He lives in what I believe to be Sandra's building? She's in the tall one? And I don't mean Neighborhood Watch, I mean 'Hood Watch."

"You guys are getting weirder by the minute."

To Stan, he said, "Get Officer Bob to maybe tell the missus what was used to uh 'kill' her husband. Maybe tell her he was found lying on the street." Xavier made eye contact with Maureen. "Sound good?"

Maureen nodded.

"And let her think that her darling husband is dead."

Maureen gasped.

"That she's the only suspect. That she's also being considered a suspect in six other cases. Oh." He pointed at Theo. "Make that seven. If you can scare her with that, she might want to put the blame where it belongs."

"Seven?" said Maureen and Stan like a pair of perfectly balanced stereo speakers. "Seven?"

"Would I lie to you?"

"Shit," said Maureen.

☺

Theo was removed from the walk-in refrigerator with subdued fanfare to be taken to what everyone had been calling The New Guy's Room, but what would now be called The Two Guys' Room. Theo was alive. Someone had indeed dosed him with zombie powder. And it had to be someone who lived in the shelter, or at least knew about the shelter. Someone in his own group. But if anybody knew anything, that "anybody" was not going to let slip that he or she knew one single bloody thing. It was now the stereotypical situation of, "Who me? No way. I don't know nothin'."

"Any word on Pamela?" Stan asked Barry on the way through the main cafeteria.

Barry had been standing there, mouth agape, beside Missus Cheffie, who was actually his wife but he could never remember that particular truth, or at least that's what he always said.

Missus Cheffie was the one who answered the question but only by shaking her head.

"Looks like you're on the job then, Barry," Stan told him. "Can you maybe come with us to the new guy's room? 'Cept now it's going to be the two guys' room. Stay with them for an hour or so? Make sure they're all right while I'm away on business? I have to go find a couple of people."

"You want this guy…" Maureen moved her head slightly in Barry's direction, "… to look after Muffy and this Theo guy? He obviously has memory issues. Why would you even think about letting him do that?"

Stan's smile was kind. "He was a paramedic for thirty-four years until the drugs took hold." To Barry, he said, "I'll be back as soon as I can."

"Oh," said Maureen.

"That part of his brain was never affected. It's about the only thing he can remember, right Cheffie?"

"That's true," she said. "I cut myself when I'm chopping something up and he's there in an instant. He's even put in sutures. I'm right as rain in five minutes max. But ask him to remember to put salt in the water when he's boiling potatoes? No. Or to even turn the stove on in the first place? No." Missus Cheffie hugged Maureen tightly. "Your boyfriend will be safe as anything—"

"He's not my fucking boyfriend!"

"—with Barry looking after him. Barry's getting better. Every day he gets better." Missus Cheffie released Maureen.

"Xavier! Tell her!"

"That's OK, dear," Missus Cheffie said. "We know he's married. We've all made mistakes. You don't need to be ashamed about being in love with somebody even though you shouldn't be."

"Oh stop."

18

"I *THOUGHT* I knew him from somewhere," said Maureen to Xavier as he set mugs of tea on the cafeteria table. Hers in front of the seat square to his. Their empty supper dishes and utensils had been piled neatly on the far corner of the table.

"Who?"

"Barry. When I saw how he was handling Muffy and Theo in that room, it came back. He used to call me Mau. Really nice guy. He had some kind of breakdown or something. Got into the booze. Can't blame him. A paramedic's job is a tough one. Then drugs, last I heard. Jeez. That'd be maybe twenty, twenty-five years ago. So he ended up here somehow, eh?"

"That was a good idea." Xavier took a sip of tea.

"What was?" Maureen sipped. "Ooh. This is nice tea!"

"For us to hang onto Muffy's phone and Health card. It's jasmine."

She frowned.

Xavier pointed to her mug. "The tea. It's jasmine. From Kowloon Market. Over on Somerset. You've never been there?"

"I've been by it a million times."

"Should give the door into the place a pull some time, like the sign on it says to do."

"If I ever escape from your evil clutches, I just might."

"Ha ha."

"Do you think she'll fall for it? That Muffy's dead?"

"I don't know why not. Officer Bob is... Well. He's good at doing what a situation calls for. She'll believe him. I think she'll tell him what we need to know. I hope so. I don't want to bring her down seaside and have Don question her."

"You're crazy if you think I'm going to believe that. It's an octopus, for fuck's sake."

"No, no. We wouldn't ask him to do that. But we might ask him to scare the information out of her. Don would probably have fun with that."

"No kidding," said Maureen without humor. "Yesterday, when I was still living in the real world, he would have scared me, but now that I've seen how well Doctor Koi has tamed him, I wouldn't be scared of him at all."

"Um. Well. To be honest, I wouldn't one hundred percent trust him."

"You're just saying that, eh? To keep me in line? In case?"

"Nope."

"I don't believe you. He seems really sweet and gentle. I would trust him. Anyway. So it's that important to find out where the uh... where she got the special substance from."

"The police know about three."

"Muffy is four."

"Theo."

"Five. But you said seven."

"So I did."

"Is that true?"

"Pamela's missing."

"Are you changing the subject?"

"Perhaps."

"What if she just went shopping like that Vinny guy said?"

"Vanni."

"Vanni." Maureen closed her eyes. "That guy's name is Vanni. That guy's name is Vanni." She opened her eyes. "I get the sense that some of the people here are scared of him or something."

"He has that effect on some people. Yes."

"You?"

"Perhaps. See... I uh... I made a mistake. He uh... Several years ago, when I was still on the streets—him, too—he approached me wanting to learn about my religion. It's such a rare occurrence, I trusted him. I taught him too much."

"Could you possibly find it in your heart to perhaps teach me this 'too much'?"

"What?"

"We have somebody turning people into zom— Shh." Maureen quieted her voice. "... into zombies. You are saying seven but I think you're lying about that."

Xavier smiled at her. "Really. You already know me well enough to be able to discern whether or not I'm lying."

She ignored him and continued. "Then we have a tame octopus that waves its tentacles around and some old lady is interpreting this like she was reading Tarot cards or something."

"They're called arms and he is the one who has been training *us* to understand *him* through sign language. He and Doctor Koi have become good friends."

A laugh escaped Maureen. "You guys are nutser than nuts. Anyway.

So we have this…" She glanced around and quieted her voice, "…zombie thing…" Her voice returned to normal. "This octopus thing, this underground sea thing and this place here…" She swept her arm out and around. "… full of elderly folks who are amazingly healthy and spry except for the one with memory issues. Well, if you include Muffy and Theo, I guess I should say except for three. And the guys here don't know about the guys down below. Except for maybe Stan? Does he know about the octopus and all that?"

"No. He doesn't know about below. Not exactly. Or maybe I should say, not entirely."

"See? There you go. Making it even more complicated and weird. Speaking of weird, you guys also have these weird elevators. And there's supposed to be something going on down there that's extremely dangerous. You've got alarms all over the place but none here. Am I right so far?"

"Not bad. Not bad at all."

"And everything seems to be a secret to the outside world. And like I said, even to each other. What's going on? Did I suffer a head injury or something?"

"Everything ties together. You're still in your right mind, dear girl."

"If that's the case, then talk."

"*Wi Madam.* But first, I'll get more tea."

"The people who live on this level are homeless—house-less—seniors who were alcoholics or drug addicts, or both, and living on the streets. Some are even ex-convicts and no, we don't discuss what they were in for. And no, this isn't a halfway house. Everyone who lives here had to earn their keep by staying clean for at least one year."

"Sounds fair enough," said Maureen.

"They also had to agree to be Guinea pigs without knowing what would be done to them."

"Honest to God, you guys are, like, over the freaking top!"

"That's the only way they will be allowed to live here. And the only way they can be as healthy as they are. You already noticed that."

"I did but I didn't put two and two together. I mean… Yeah. These guys were homeless street people and on drugs and booze for years and they don't… seem… to have a single health issue going on. Clear complexions. And they're my age but hardly any wrinkles. What, uh…?"

"You asked. You sure you want to know?"

"I think so. What are my options?"

"Only one option, dear girl. You must never, ever, ever tell anyone."

"Or?"

"You might find out what it feels like to be turned into a zombie. Or eaten by worse than an octopus."

"Is that a threat?"

Without any perceivable expression on his face, Xavier stared at her from under his eyebrows.

"Or a promise?"

"Your choice," he said.

"All right. I'll keep my mouth shut. That's something we have to do as medical professionals anyway. A patient is entitled to privacy so I will start thinking of everyone around as being a patient."

"Good girl."

"Don't call me that. I'm not a puppy."

"Sorry. They still go to the surface like they did in the old days, but they tend not to hang out with the same people. They shop for us. They run errands. They build projects in our seaside resort down below, but they don't know that's where they are when they're doing it. We lie to them about where they are and use blindfolds and earplugs. You've seen some of their work. One of the men, since deceased, organized the building of those huge steel doors you passed through when you first got here. Pamela was the one in charge of the office partitions. Not the building of them, the painting."

"She's good."

"She is. She was a nurse's aide in her day—among many other things—so helps out with… certain projects, but stays completely out of the limelight. Abusive ex."

"At her age? Still?"

"She's sixty. Looks a lot older because of… Well. What he did to her. He's younger by a few years. We're working on getting her face regenerated but it's taking its time."

"You do plastic surgery here?"

Xavier shook his head. "I didn't say renovated, I said regenerated."

"You mean as in…"

"Yes. As in what many sea creatures can do. They can regrow limbs, internal organs, even brains. Humans can regrow skin, as you know. And the liver. But that's about all humans can do. We've just uh… bumped it up a notch here."

"A notch."

"A few notches."

"Shit."

"And that's why we need to find out who's turning people into… If the police find out about the…" Xavier glanced around the empty cafeteria and lowered his voice. "… the zombie powder, they'll blame me. They know me. They know what I do every Saturday night."

"Just when I thought it couldn't get any more complicated, you throw in another twist. What, pray tell, do you do every Saturday night."

"I actually am a Vodou Master, a priest, and I hold services every Saturday evening at a place on Montreal Road. There's another religious group rents part of a building there and they hold their services on Sunday mornings. Because Haitian Vodou has elements of Catholicism, these people let me use their place. The cops watch both of our groups like we were members of some Islamic terrorist cult. White cops. Christian cops.

Superstitious, suspicious cops."

"And these cops will assume you're the one who's making the zombies."

"You got it."

"But you're not. Are you?"

"Would I lie to you?"

"I think you would, but I don't think you are right now. So, like, uh… Then what? What if they arrest you?"

"The only way I can prove I'm not turning people into zombies is to let the police go below. And we can't have that. Not ever."

Maureen raised her eyebrows.

"The entire world down there would be destroyed in no time. You know what some people are like."

"Greedy as hell."

"Greedy as hell. They'd be in there taking over and claiming it all as their own and selling everything. They'd open it up to have free and easy access. Everything would become just as polluted as it is on the surface. There would be wars upon wars upon wars while they attempted to keep possession of that entire world while others tried to wrest it from them. Everything would be destroyed. Everything would die. Exactly like what's been going on for millennia in what you call the real world."

"I hear you."

"But there's more to it than that. We have a… Shall we call it an 'issue' on our end of things, too?"

"What issue would that be?"

"Remember those men we hid from when you first got through the wooden door?"

"Yes."

"And how they were saying someone disappeared around there?"

"Yes."

"Nobody's going to find that body. That guy is gone. Not a shred left of him."

"Oh. Something ate him? Was it that big monster from under the sea you told me about? You said it was highly intelligent or something?"

"Nope. That thing is not exactly what they call 'the least of one's worries' but in comparison—"

A movement beside them made both Maureen and Xavier jump.

It was Doctor Koi, holding out her cell phone to Xavier.

Sandra and Tovy, with worried faces, stood near her.

"We have to go below."

"What's wrong?"

"I just got an urgent message from Don. Look." She held out her cell phone.

Texted were three lines:

000

707

000

"What does that mean?' asked Maureen. "And how can he text?"

"All is clear. S.O.S. All is clear."

"Sounds a mite contradictory to me," said Sandra with a brief hello-wave and slight smile at Maureen.

"That's an extra reason we have to go back. Let's go."

"But how can he do that?"

"He helped rig up a system where he just has to poke the tip of an arm against the rock outside my apartment," said Doctor Koi. "How do you think we can get Internet service two thousand feet below sea level through solid rock? The guy's a genius. Well. His uh, his connections are geniuses. Or would that be genii?"

Maureen's mouth opened with a question, but she shut it again and shook her head.

"Lead on, MacDuff," said Tovy.

Tapping her cell phone, Doctor Koi led the way.

"I'll catch up to you later," said Xavier. "I need to get Theo started on meds. Et cetera."

He blew Maureen a kiss.

She rolled her eyes.

19

WITH WHAT APPEARED to be overdone caution, Doctor Koi touched the wall beside the opening to the patio outside her apartment. The huge, darkened glass window rose.

There, partly on and partly hanging off the patio, was Don. Flat and unmoving. Gray as the stone beneath him.

Doctor Koi rushed to kneel beside him. "Don. Don. I'm here. What's wrong? What happened?"

The tip of the arm on the left side of his head moved slightly.

Maureen, face pale, said, "It looks like he's missing a couple of his arm things." She pointed.

Doctor Koi reached over Don to roll him slightly toward her. She withdrew her hand. It was covered in blue. "Oh, no. He's bleeding."

"Blue blood? Those things have blue blood?"

"Don't just stand there. You're an ER nurse. Do something."

"You're the marine biologist. *You* do something."

Sandra, who was standing beside Maureen, said, "Where's the first aid kit?"

"We don't use those anymore here," said Tovy, face reddening.

"What? You're digging out tunnels and nobody ever gets hurt? I can't believe this place. You're right, Maureen. They're all nuts."

"We aren't the ones smoothing out the tunnels."

"Oh my God," said Maureen, coming to her senses. "Where's the kitchen? Do you have any supplies down here? Give me a towel or something."

Tovy darted into the room beside the barred door. He returned with two towels.

Maureen snatched them from him and dropped to her knees beside Doctor Koi. "Turn him over this way a bit more, if you can." She placed one towel on the exposed area where Don's arms had been severed. "Looks like they've been cut off."

"Bitten off more likely," said Tovy. "Look."

About thirty feet from the patio, a huge creature bobbed belly up at the surface of the water.

"You got him," whispered Doctor Koi.

Don responded with a flutter of eye and a flick of the left arm beside it.

"He got it," she said. "He finally got it."

Don squeezed that eye closed and seemingly with great effort, raised that left arm higher.

"Do you think maybe he's saying no?" asked Maureen. "It's like he's trying to tell you something."

Don flicked his right arm.

"Looks like whatever that thing is, got him back."

Don flicked his left arm.

"Keep applying pressure to that. Do you have any honey?"

"Honey?" said Tovy. "Always. I have some in my digs." He ran out.

"So do I—" Doctor Koi said, too late to stop Tovy from exiting.

"What's honey going to do?" asked Sandra.

"Perform a miracle, I hope. Scissors? Where are your scissors?"

"Behind the bar," said Doctor Koi.

Sandra was already on her way.

"Top drawer on the right."

Tovy ran in with a half-full jar of golden-brown liquid. "Got it."

"Scissors," said Sandra, handing them to Maureen.

"Here." Maureen handed them back to her. She rose to her feet. "Cut the bottom of my dress off. Doctor Koi? Maintain the pressure but get ready to remove the towel."

Sandra was halfway around Maureen's dress. "What *is* that thing floating out there, Doc?"

"Looks like it could be an ichthyosaur. But it's way bigger than I've ever heard of, so maybe not. You never know about anything down here. Hurry up."

Maureen stepped aside as the last bit of the bottom of her dress hit the floor. "Good. Now we are going to make a kind of gauze-ish pressure bandage and tie it around him to keep the honey where we want it."

"You want me to cut this in half lengthwise then?" asked Sandra.

"Yes. And tie the ends together. To make one long piece." At this, Maureen slid into the water off the patio. "I'll uh… I hope he doesn't mind me feeling around underneath him. Don't they have some kind of stabby thing they kill with?"

"It's called a beak and I doubt very much if he's going to attack you with it."

"Ready with the honey," said Tovy, holding the now-lidless jar over Don's injured area.

Sandra handed the long strip of Maureen's dress down to her.

Maureen took one end of it and holding her breath, dove under the water. On the other side of Don, near Doctor Koi, Maureen's hand with one end of the long strip of cloth in it came up.

Sandra snatched it and pulled, slowly and gently.

Maureen popped up from the water with the other end of the cloth wrapped across her shoulders to hang down in front of her. "Help me out."

Tovy handed the jar of honey to Doctor Koi and he and Sandra lifted Maureen from the water.

Tovy took the jar of honey back.

Sandra smoothed the makeshift pressure bandage out.

"Grab the other towel," ordered Maureen.

Tovy had it in his free hand almost instantly.

"Ready?" she asked Doctor Koi, who had both hands on her towel again.

Doctor Koi nodded.

"Lift off your towel."

Doctor Koi did and threw it aside.

"Pour."

Tovy poured honey.

"Towel."

Tovy handed the towel to Doctor Koi who placed it over Don's wounds.

Maureen then pulled her end of the strip of cloth from her shoulders and snatched the other end of it from Sandra's hand in what looked like one single move.

A knot was tied in seconds.

Maureen slumped to the patio floor. "Ah. There. Now let's hope it works. Poor wee doll. Oh. Poor big doll, I guess."

Slowly, two of Don's arms slid together to form a heart shape, then they flopped to the patio floor alongside Maureen. But one of them snaked out again to slide over to her cheek and caress it.

A happy tune came from the small purse Doctor Koi still had hanging across her shoulder. She pulled out her cell phone, tapped it, and squeezed her face as she groaned, "Oh, no. Xavier needs us. We gotta go."

"What's wrong?" asked Tovy. "What about Don?"

Doctor Koi shook her head, her face still squeezed with worry. "A breach."

"I'm guessing not as in a birth?" said Maureen.

"And you'd be right." Doctor Koi stuffed her phone back into her purse and headed toward the bar. She rummaged around behind it for a moment and came out with a plastic gun. A taser. This, she slid into her purse. "Let's go. Sandra? You, too. We have to leave you alone, Maureen." She pointed to the wall beside the open window. "Use Don's cell phone if you need to contact me."

"What?"

Tovy had disappeared and was now waiting outside Doctor Koi's open entrance door.

One of Don's arms snaked out to grab Maureen by the chin. He turned her to face him. His right arm went up.

"He knows how to operate his cell phone," said Doctor Koi. "He'll show you."

Maureen glanced at the stone wall, then at Don.

Don's right arm rose. *Yes.*

Maureen rose to her feet. "OK then, but what about that thing out there? It's dead, I guess, eh? It's not going to come back in and attack Don again?"

As Doctor Koi followed Sandra out the door, she turned to say, "I hope not. We'll try to get back as soon as we can."

Tovy called out, "Hurry up."

She continued. "We'll bring some supplies. Stan will know what we need. Looks like he's going to find out what's been going on down here."

"I wish I had my cell phone," said Maureen.

"Oh. I have it. Rocky gave it to me," said Tovy, setting it on the floor just inside the doorway. "But it won't work. Don has to set it up for you. And close this door."

Maureen turned to look down at Don who flicked the right-arm yes signal at her.

"All the more reason to do your best to keep him conscious, right?"

Maureen grunted. "That's what I do. But it's usually only for humans."

Don tapped her side and when she turned, he had formed a smile under his eyes.

20

MAUREEN WAS SEATED on the patio beside Don, her legs dangling in the water beside three of his arms.

"So," she said. "I have no idea what the pain tolerance of an octopus might be but is it feeling any better with the honey treatment?"

Don raised his right arm closest to his face.

"That really does mean yes?"

He flicked it again.

"What's no, then?"

He flicked his left arm closest to his face.

"Ah." She smiled. "So it's true then. You can understand what we say to you?"

Right arm. Left arm. Right arm. Left arm.

"Is that a maybe? Or sometimes? Or something like that?"

Right arm. Then this right arm snaked out to tap Maureen's arm. It then pointed out to the floating creature. Two arms formed a heart and one of them pointed again at the creature.

"You're saying you like this creature? But why? It attacked you."

Left arm.

"It didn't?"

Right arm. Then again, a heart and pointing. But this time, the pointing hand made a motion of drawing inward. Drawing inward again.

"You want me to bring that thing in?"

Right arm. Heart. Right arm.

"But it attacked you. It bit off your arms."

Left arm.

"It didn't?"

Right arm.

"Then who did?"

Don pointed downward into the water then underneath his body then downward again.

Maureen laughed. "Are you saying... Sorry for laughing and forgive me if I'm wrong, but..."

Right arm. Heart.

"Are you saying it was some asshole from down there who attacked you?"

Right arm.

"Did it attack that creature out there?"

Right arm.

"Oh. Wow. OK. Um. How can I get it in here, then?"

Don pointed along the patio toward a turn that would have led to her own apartment's patio.

"I can find something there?"

Right arm.

She climbed back up onto the patio and cautiously moved along the rock wall to look around the bend.

Just under that patio's overhang sat a boat. A boat with a net and a huge coil of rope attached to it. The rope was firmly knotted into a metal ring at the boat's stern. "Found it."

Maureen was able to get the boat out to the huge creature who was floating belly up. When she moved around to the far side of it, she knew immediately that it had been attacked by something even bigger than it was.

"Was it some kind of giant shark that attacked you guys?" she called out.

Don formed a question mark.

"Do you know what a shark is?"

Yes.

"Oh. So you don't know what it was."

Yes.

"It was big, though, right?"

Yes. Don's skin flashed bright red, orange and yellow then went back to the gray of the patio.

"Does that mean it was scary?"

Yes.

By this time, Maureen had managed to get the net around what would be the upper chest and arms of the creature. She secured it by knotting the rope through one of the openings. "Ready, set, go."

She pulled on the boat's oars and although the creature she was hauling was huge, within several pulls, she was at the patio.

"It bit a hole in your friend's side." She climbed out of the boat while Don held it with one of his arms. "You OK holding that?"

She waited.

"Oh. Sorry. Your right hand is occupied."

With another of his arms, Don formed a smile.

"I'll be right back."

In no time, Maureen had secured honey, scissored sheets, and a towel, and Don's friend was wrapped and resuming consciousness.

"How do you guys communicate?" she asked. "He only has those paddle-ish flipper things."

Something rumbled. The patio seemed to almost vibrate.

Don reached out to grasp Maureen's hand which he placed on the neck of the creature.

A rumble of sound but under Maureen's hand, vibrations.

"Oh. I think I know. You can talk to each other but it's below the level of human hearing?"

The creature's throat vibrated. Don flipped his right arm.

"That is totally cool! Do all the creatures down here talk like that?"

Yes. No. Yes. No.

"Only some."

Yes.

"How about the uh… the asshole down below? Does he talk?"

Maureen still had her hand on the creature's neck so was almost pushed off the patio when it thrashed and whirled and threw its paddle-like flippers under the water and out again. It righted itself.

A rumble.

Maureen reached out to put her hand on Don. She could feel purring.

The creature calmed.

She readjusted the creature's makeshift bandages then settled herself on the patio with her legs dangling down between the arms of Don and the head and neck of his friend.

21

XAVIER, DOCTOR KOI and Tovy had returned in a panicked rush only to run out at the same speed when they saw Don's creature friend at the edge of the patio alongside Maureen's legs that still dangled over the patio. She was sipping from a bottle of water.

Maureen smiled, "Did you just roll your eyes at them, Don?"

Right arm.

"You're funny. I wish you were human."

Don's remaining arms made signals as, behind Maureen, Doctor Koi, in a subdued voice, said, "He just said, 'I wish you were an octopus.' Why is that familiar?"

Maureen lifted her feet out of the water and rose to her feet. "Maybe the Beatles? 'I'd like to be under the sea in an octopus's garden in the shade.'"

"Ah, yes. That's it. I liked that song. It's about the only one of theirs I did like. I was more into Peggy Lee and Billie Holiday."

Behind her, Tovy and Xavier approached cautiously.

"Is it dead?" asked Tovy.

"It's a friend of Don's. They were both injured in a fight with something from down below. Don called it an asshole."

A flurry of Don's remaining arms made Maureen's face redden to about the same color as Don's body had flashed for a moment.

"Sorry. He called it a vent, not an asshole."

Don's arms formed a heart.

"I see you've made friends with him."

"It wasn't difficult." Maureen formed a heart at Don. "Where's the first aid kit? You brought one?"

"We did better than that," said Xavier, stepping aside to indicate the man just now struggling through the doorway with a bulging knapsack. "We brought an entire doctor with us. You've met Stan?"

"The vet! Perfect. Hey Don. We got you an animal doctor. He'll fix you up... What's he saying, Doctor Koi?"

"He's wondering why you brought an animal doctor to see to him and... uh... I can't quite make out what his friend's name is. He says they aren't animals."

A rumble.

"Oh, wait. His friend doesn't have a name. He wants us to give it one." She smiled at Maureen. "Any ideas?"

"Is it male?"

Right arm, Yes.

"How about Apollo then? Poseidon? Apollo?"

"Excellent," said Xavier. "We're in Little Italy. We can call it Paulo. What do you think, Don?"

Right arm, Yes. A smile emoji below Don's eyes.

The right flipper of the creature caressed its own head.

Don waved and curled his arms again.

"Don says that Paulo can understand most of what we say, but can't communicate with us except through Don." Doctor Koi paused as Don continued. "'Anything you need him to do, it's best that you tell me and I'll tell him. And vice versa.' He says, that way there won't be any misunderstandings."

"How can he do that?" asked Stan, pulling out instruments, bottles and clear-film-wrapped cloths from the knapsack. "He's an octopus."

"They can talk to each other," said Maureen. "… but it's below our hearing frequency." She turned to Don again. "Does the vent talk, too?"

Right arm. Left arm. Right arm. Left arm. Then a flurry of circular motions and stabs into the air.

Doctor Koi translated. "He says, 'I don't know. If it does make sounds, we can't hear them. We call it Sunshine because we know the sun exists, but we've never seen it. And because apparently the sun can be dangerous… But only to those living on the Surface. Right? Please tell me the sun's not dangerous for us down here.'"

By this time, Stan was peeking under the makeshift bandage Maureen had tied around Don. "Excellent. Excellent. And it looks like regeneration has already begun."

"That fast?" asked Maureen. "And I don't think you have to worry about the sun way down here, you guys."

"Are you certain the injury happened only hours ago?"

"Yes," said Doctor Koi. "As you can probably guess, we are in an entirely unique biosphere here. Things are very, very different. Very different." She leaned down to caress Don's head.

"So it seems." With surprisingly gentle hands, Stan lifted the honey-soaked towel from Don's wound then slipped the strip of Maureen's cut-off dress from around him.

He handed this back to Doctor Koi who untied the other knot and rinsed the dress parts off in the water before handing them to Maureen. "I have needle and thread if you want."

"Sandra's the expert with that stuff, not— Hey. Where is she?"

"Calm down, calm down," Xavier was at Maureen's side almost instantly. "We left her Topside."

"You fucking bastards. You let her go but you're keeping me trapped down here! How fair is that?"

A rumble. Then from the water around them, a series of barely audible murmurings and giggling bubbles from Don to Paulo and back.

"Oh, dear girl. We left her with Barry. She volunteered to help out with Theo and Muffy. *She* is willing to help us out without questioning our motives."

Maureen huffed and squatted down beside Stan who was now tending to Paulo's wound. It was already scabbing over.

Stan removed the strip of makeshift bandage and held that out to Maureen, but Doctor Koi snatched it from his hand and washed it off before handing this to Maureen, too.

"That's a chunk of your draperies, Doctor Koi. Not sure a needle and thread will do justice to them."

"I'll get the manufacturer to repair them. Don? Will you send out a signal, please? Too bad you have such a distaste for arachnids, Maureen. She'd be happy to fix your skirt for you."

"*Ew!*" The strip of cut-up draperies dropped from Maureen's hand instantly. "That's made of spider webs?" She stood to move away from it.

"Not exactly your—" Doctor Koi covered her mouth but the smile in her eyes was not so easily hidden. "They're not exactly your 'garden variety' spider. They're an aquatic species. Amphibians, actually. They…" She looked closely at Maureen's face. "Are you all right?"

"You mean there are spiders in here? Like, all over the walls and everything?"

"You want this net?" asked Stan. "It's got a tear in it but otherwise looks good." He waved it at Doctor Koi.

"That's mine," said Tovy. "I'll take it to the…" He laughed. "… the manufacturer for repairs."

"That's not the least bit funny," said Maureen, rubbing her hands onto what was left of her dress.

Another rumble and giggling bubbles from the water around Don and Paulo.

"You guys are mean. All of you." Maureen made a move toward the apartment doorway.

"Wait, Maureen. Wait." Xavier had his hand on her arm. "You're part of us now. Part of the team. You need to know what's going on."

"I wouldn't mind an update, too," said Stan, tucking instruments and packages back into his knapsack. "This place is an absolute treasure trove of potential."

"And that, ladies and germs," said Xavier, "is the problem."

22

"**WE HAVE BAD** news," Xavier began. "We've been invaded."

A flurry of arms and flippers in the water.

"They got into Topside. Not down here. So far we're OK here."

Don's skin returned to neutral gray and Paulo's flippers flattened out on the water's surface.

"But. This means, unfortunately, that we will have two new citizens. Two Surface men who will have to be indoctrinated into our way of life and never allowed out again."

At this, Maureen gasped. "Is that what I am actually facing? And my friend Sandra? Are we to be trapped in here forever, too?"

Xavier's smile was kind. "You have more to hide than I have, dear girl. You could probably leave right now if you wished to. However, I would like to call upon your inner-nurse kindness and beg you to stay with us for at least a while. We need you. We need Sandra, too."

Don formed a heart. Paulo caressed his own head with his right flipper.

"As you see, I'm not the only one who likes you and wants you to stay."

A flurry of octopus arms.

Doctor Koi interpreted. "'But only if you wish.'"

"What exactly do you need *me* for? And Sandra? You guys seem to have been doing just fine for… How many years now? Ten? Fifteen?"

"Twenty," said Tovy.

"Twenty some," said Xavier.

"Twenty some for me as well," said Doctor Koi. "And twenty some for Rocky. He and Xavier were the first ones down here."

A flurry of splashing.

"Sorry. The first humans down here."

Don formed a smile. Paulo caressed his own head again.

"We don't want to bring Officer Bob into this just yet. We don't want to open that can of worms until we have to. So I'm wondering—we're wondering—if you wouldn't mind helping us out with the interview. I mean, all those TV crime shows you watch must have given you some idea how to get information out of a suspect. Even though you're not officially—or legally—trained for it, I think you could pull it off."

Don raised his right arm straight into the air and flapped about a hand-sized portion of it several times.

"I'm sorry, Don, but no. Not this time. At least, not yet. If Maureen can't get the information out of them, we will consider letting you take a shot at it. But remember what happened last time! We can't have that!"

Don formed a smile.

"And it wasn't funny."

Don placed two of his arms to form a laugh emoji.

"*Onèt bay Bondye*, honest to God, Don, sometimes…"

Don formed a heart.

Xavier shook his head as his eyes looked upwards. "All right. That's settled then. Let's head up to Topside and—"

"Um. Excuse me," said Maureen. "I didn't hear myself agreeing to this."

"That's beside the point," said Xavier, smiling and gently grasping her upper arm. "We don't need your agreement. We need your expertise. Let's go."

"Listen. This boss-Maureen-around shit has to stop. And right now!" She attempted to pull her arm away from Xavier, without success.

Two beeps from Xavier's pocket caused him to let her go so he could reach for his cell phone. "*Bonjou.*" He listened for a moment. He thumbed off his phone. He slipped it into his pocket. "*Kaka.*"

"What?" said Tovy, "They found Pamela? Is she…?"

"The men escaped."

"Back to the Surface?"

"Apparently not. They're probably on the way down here. That was Barry. He said they went through the wall. He's all freaked out. Afraid he's imagining things. Like walls moving. Poor bugger. For once he's not hallucinating. And for once I'm happy that his memory's no good."

"Let's go meet them then," said Tovy. "With blasters. That elevator door opens and we got 'em. Pow. Fried."

"They took Sandra hostage."

Maureen's "Shit" was echoed by Tovy's and Doctor Koi's.

It had taken some convincing on Don's part, but Xavier and Doctor Koi had finally agreed to let him accompany them to the elevator where the two men and Sandra would be arriving shortly. There would be no "frying" of anyone. There would be a capture of one by Don, who would take the man on the left as the door opened, and the other by the combination of Xavier and Tovy, who would take the man on the right. Maureen and Doctor Koi would grab Sandra—who, they hoped, would be between the men—and get her safely away to Doctor Koi's apartment.

Stan would inject the men with an anesthetic, and they would be locked away until it was time for their "interview."

23

"ALL RIGHT," SAID Xavier. "They have food and water for when they wake up. There's nothing they can use for a weapon in there. There's no way they can get out." He paused. "Let's hope nothing will get in."

With eyebrows raised and eyes widened, Tovy muttered and nodded.

"So, we can all just relax—more or less—as we try to figure out what's next. As in, what are we going to do with these guys now that they know how to get all the way down here? And how are we going to prevent them from telling anybody else about this world if—IF—we let them go?"

Tovy said, "Best bet would be to feed them to the fishes."

"I wouldn't want the poor fishes to be consuming anything that might be inside those men," said Doctor Koi. "Like that drug Stan gave them for one thing. And…" She waved her hand back and forth past her nose. "… the stench of alcohol off them is enough to get me drunk just breathing it in. We'd have to wait until their systems clear."

Stan laughed. "You guys are funny." Then his face went serious. "You *are* joking. Right?"

Xavier patted Stan's shoulder. "That might end up being our only option."

"What?" said Maureen. "Are you seriously thinking of killing those guys?"

"You can't," added Sandra. "That's murder."

"We might not have a choice," said Doctor Koi.

Maureen and Sandra exchanged wide-eyed glances and when they turned to Stan, he merely shrugged at them.

"But first," said Xavier. "I want to find out who the hell showed them how to get into Topside in the first place. That should be our main concern. That person is the one who needs to be fed to the fishes. Oh!" Xavier plucked his cell phone from his pocket. "*Bonjou.*"

Xavier listened for several moments, muttered a *mèsi*, then returned his phone to his pocket.

"That was Rocky. Muffy's wife isn't home. Apparently, she's gone on some overnight yacht adventure with some other hard-done-by wives."

Maureen cleared her throat.

"I'm just quoting Rocky who was just quoting Officer Bob. Don't blame me for the phraseology."

"And this means…?" asked Tovy.

"This *could* mean that we would be able to take it easy for the night. Get some much-needed sleep. Let our captives stew. However, according to Officer Bob, one of the men we have with us is none other than Pamela's abusive ex-husband, Billy."

"How the hell could he know that?" demanded Maureen. "I didn't think you were going to… How did you put it? Bring him in on this."

Xavier's half-controlled smile asked Maureen, *How indeed?* "All right, people. Let's get this place set up for our first interview. I hope you're fine with our using your place, Doctor Koi?"

"Best place if we want to have Don involved. Right, Don?"

Don flipped his right arm, *Yes*.

Still beside him, Paulo tapped the water gently with the flat of his right flipper.

"Excuse me," said Stan. "If Sandra is down here that means Barry is alone Topside with our patients. Right?"

"Good point," said Xavier.

"Best I get back up there to check on things," said Stan.

"Another good point."

"And… a third good point is that those guys are going to be completely out of it, in one form or another, for probably five or six hours depending on how much they've had to drink. Combine that with what I gave them, and they might be confused for even longer."

"Where have I heard that concept before," said Maureen to no one in particular.

"Maybe confused enough that we don't need to worry about feeding them to anything."

"I'll go with you," said Sandra. "I was in the middle of a job interview when they grabbed me."

Maureen laughed. "A what?"

"Missus Cheffie likes the idea of Barry helping out in the Two Guys' Room. Says it's helping him think and concentrate. With Theo out of it too, she's looking for a temporary sous chef slash server."

"Do you have any idea what you'd be in for?" asked Xavier. "That's not an easy job. Especially with Missus Cheffie as your boss. I wouldn't do it for love nor money." He smiled at Maureen. "Nope. Not even for you, dear girl."

Maureen rolled her eyes.

"It would only be temporary. Until they find Pamela. Then I can help in the… Missus Cheffie wants to call it the hospital. She trains me, Stan trains me, and I can help in both places. Whenever I'm needed."

"I think that would be wonderful," said Stan.

"Perfect," said Xavier. "That's settled. Until tomorrow morning—early tomorrow morning—try to relax and get some sleep. And we'll see you all then." He took Maureen's arm. "Let's get you tucked in for the night. You're going to be busy tomorrow, dear girl."

"Stop calling me girl. I'm a woman, for Christ's sake."

"She's all yours, Xavier," Sandra laughed. "Have fun."

Then she hooked arms with Stan and out the door they went.

"Doctor Koi? I recommend you have Tovy stay in your apartment tonight. For safety reasons. I've got a feeling we're going to be dealing with a lot more than just a couple of new guys. I'll be staying with Maureen."

Maureen's mouth flew open. "Oh really! You think you can just boss me around. What have I told you about that?"

Xavier ignored her. "After the draperies are repaired, I recommend you still keep them open so you and Don can keep an eye on each other."

Don raised his right arm. Beside him, Paulo's right flipper raised.

"That I will, Xavier. That I will." Turning to Tovy, Doctor Koi said, "Up for a game of chess? Winner gets the bed? Loser gets the sofa?"

"You are on, Doc."

A flurry of splashes made everyone turn toward Don.

Doctor Koi said, "No. You have to play against the winner. Challenge yourself, Don. One cannot improve by beating losers all the time."

A single, large bubble rose from underneath Don's body.

"What's that mean?" asked Maureen.

Xavier smiled as he tugged on Maureen's arm to pull her along out the door with him. "Looks like he's starting to pick up some of your vocabulary, dear girl."

Don formed a laugh emoji below his eyes then turned that into a heart shape at Maureen's disappearing back.

24

THE NIGHT WAS uneventful. Maureen had fallen asleep almost the moment Xavier had turned off the lights. Xavier, lying back in the leather La-Z-Boy in the TV area, had stayed awake for nearly an hour, face pinched with concern, until he, too, had finally dozed off.

Come morning, though, things were different. A banging from the other side of the door that was braced by the wooden bar in the metal holders woke them both in a panic.

"What the hell is going on?" asked Maureen. "What's doing that?"

Xavier had Maureen by the hand and out her door within seconds. He slammed it closed behind them. They ran past the small drawing of the pebble, then past Tovy's apartment door with its tiny volcano label.

"Doctor Koi. Tovy. Doctor Koi. Tovy," he called out. "Let us in."

The entrance panel slid open to reveal, at floor level, several pale, surfboard-like creatures with six bone-white legs. Like cheerleaders' pompoms, frilly, pink gills stuck out from each side of what was probably their necks. These fluttered with continuous motion. Pincer-like sideways jaws jutted forward below two tiny black dots, eyes. The head of the creature at the front of the group was different. Its sideways bear-trap jaws opened. It snarled at Maureen.

"What are they?" whispered Maureen at the threshold of Doctor Koi's apartment.

Her voice seemed to trigger a reaction from the creature behind the one with the bear-trap jaws. Its antennas first flipped here, then there, then pointing in her direction. A hum filled the air as it moved toward her. Maureen attempted to take a step back but Xavier's arm stopped her. The one with the bear-trap jaws, antennas flipping, retreated to the back of the group. There were eight of them.

From the water, a splashing. Don.

Almost as one, the creatures' antennas turned toward that commotion, but their eyes and bodies remained pointed at Maureen and Xavier.

"You might as well tell me what they are. I don't think I can be shocked any more than I already have been. I mean, walking ironing boards?" She laughed. "Is this a joke?"

The antennas faced forward again.

"They can understand us?"

Hand poised near the wall beside the entrance, Doctor Koi spoke. "Get inside. Let me close this. Where there's one, there are several and when there are several, there are… Well. I prefer to have them where I can see them and not coming at me from behind."

"Peachy."

Doctor Koi tapped the wall and the panel sighed closed behind Maureen and Xavier. "For want of a better name, we call them termants."

"Termants."

"I have no idea what they call themselves," said Doctor Koi. "Or even if they do. But they are an exceptionally organized and intelligent species. They're kind of a cross between a termite and an ant. I think we can throw in bee, too. In the absence of wood and other vegetation that Surface termite species live on, these guys eat rock."

Except for the fluttering of their cheerleader pompoms, the creatures were unmoving. Not a twitch of antenna among them.

"Somehow their systems are able to extract what nutrients are available in the rock. Tovy can probably help you out with that. If you're at all interested in what volcanic rocks are made of. Right, Tovy?"

Tovy, on a step ladder by the patio, was re-attaching the repaired draperies. "Sure. Be more than pleased to do that for you. Just say the word."

"Of course, they also eat aquatic creatures. Like small fish and uh… That's why I know anything at all about them. But when their young emerge from the eggs, they require a diet of—"

"Hey. Listen to her," said Xavier, grabbing hold of Doctor Koi's arm, and none too gently. "Always the lecturing scientist. You needn't keep going on about the diet of our dear friends, the termants, do you?"

Doctor Koi turned away. "And they have nests everywhere. The lava tubes are their territory. They consider this entire area to be their territory. Both aquatic and non-aquatic. We are squatters."

Xavier's attention was still on Doctor Koi so he didn't notice the frown on Maureen's face. But Tovy did.

"We'll explain about that later, too," Tovy said. Then holding one hand up alongside his mouth to hide it from the termants, he mouthed at Maureen the words: *Not in front of them.*

Maureen's face showed nothing, but the slight nod of her head told Tovy she understood.

Xavier caught this and released Doctor Koi's arm to return to Maureen's side.

"Do they visit with you on a regular basis? Are they friends like Don is?"

"Not exactly," said Doctor Koi. "Every now and again they drop in for a chat."

"Oh. You can have conversations with them?"

"You could say that. Their antennae pick up vibrations of sight and sound. That much I know. But if you think about it, our own ears operate on the basis of vibration, too."

"Huh." A slight smile touched Maureen's lips. "That's true. Yes. I never thought about it like that but, yes. Well, I did. I mean, I know that. I'm a nurse. I need to know that shit, but... Oh. These guys... These... Oh."

Xavier squeezed Maureen's arm. Hard. "Shut up."

"Ow, fuck."

"Shut up."

Doctor Koi continued. "The more I find down here, the more I'm flabbergasted. We uh... I'm sorry, but can you brace yourself for something else?"

"Sure. What could be worse than—?" Her eyes once again went to Tovy who was holding his index finger against his lips. "Uh. Sure. Let's do that then. Yes."

One of Xavier's arms snaked across Maureen's shoulders. "Just realize that she won't hurt you. She'll be more afraid of you. She doesn't know you." He squeezed Maureen closer to himself. "She translates for them to Don and Don, of course, to us. We... uh..." His eyes went to Doctor Koi's then to Tovy's. "We believe they understand us when we speak. Ready?"

"Like I said, sure. Why not?"

Doctor Koi called out, "Madame Chanel? It's OK. You can come down now."

"Madame Chanel?"

"We call her Coco."

Maureen's nervous laugh was cut short when four legs the size of pool cues poked down from the area above the patio. The pool cues each bent in two places and down dropped the rest of the creature. The other four legs of the creature. A fuzzy, sideways hourglass with eight legs, two rows of shiny eyes, and a big fuzzy belly underneath it. This was not another eight-armed octopus like Don. This was a spider.

It bounced there.

Maureen screamed.

The spider retreated onto the top of Don's body.

No movement from the termants. None whatsoever.

"It's OK, Coco," said Doctor Koi. "She won't hurt you."

The spider slowly stepped back onto the patio, to one side. There, she tapped three of her feet several times at Don.

Don translated.

Doctor Koi translated for Don.

"'You didn't tell me an outsider would be here. Oh, why do I agree to do this for you all the time? I'm terrified of humans.'"

"You're doing this because you are kind," said Doctor Koi. She turned to Maureen. "As you might have guessed, this is our textiles manufacturer. Be assured, she won't hurt you either." She turned back to Coco. "What are the termants going on about this time?"

Maureen's eyes widened as her lips formed the words *This time?*

"They don't seem pleased. At all. Have you heard anything?"

Taps of spider feet and flailing of octopus arms and Doctor Koi once again translated.

"It seems there is a... Uh. I don't know that word. There's a whatever in one of the blocked-off Surface lava tubes. And it's not blocked off at the Surface side anymore. It's been widened. Considerably widened."

Doctor Koi turned to Maureen. "I think I might know the one they're talking about. It could be the one they blocked off themselves when they accidentally broke through during construction several years ago."

"Construction?"

"Patience, Grasshopper," Xavier whispered into her ear. "We'll explain later. Do your best to keep your mouth shut."

"I—"

Through his teeth, Xavier said, "Do I have to slap my hand over your mouth again? I don't want to do that. They might then consider you a threat if I do that. Carry on, Doctor Koi. Please."

"A threa—"

Whispered: "Shhhhut up."

Doctor Koi closed her eyes for a moment, "Where was I? A yes. Inconspicuous opening at Surface level. But well-camouflaged. Previously well-camouflaged. Or so they believed. It's cave-like once inside and not a direct drop so that's why the… the *whatever*'s damages weren't terribly severe. The termants are very angry about this. They don't want any more… I don't know that word, Don… any *whatevers* coming around and messing with their homes. Especially their nests. Or even getting close to their nests. And this whatever has gotten too close. Something must be done."

A flurry of Don's arms that Doctor Koi translated as "'I don't know the word they are using either. I'll just use 'creature.' I think it's an expletive.'"

Coco tapped.

Don's arms waved.

From the area of the termants, tapping legs and flipping antennas.

"The creature they're talking about has bumps on the front of it. Sounds like they're talking about a human female, but they're refusing to call it that. They must be some ticked off about this situation. They're usually a lot more open and as far as I can remember have never described humans like this. About the bumps, especially."

Fast flickering of the antennas and tapping of legs of all the termants caused Doctor Koi to smile.

"It looks like they're laughing. They say the bumps on the front of it aren't as big as that one's there." With one leg, Coco pointed to the area of Maureen's chest.

Maureen's arms crossed her bosom. "Those things are talking about my breasts?"

"Seems so, eh?" answered Xavier, but without even the slightest hint of humor. In fact, he appeared nervous.

"They're saying another creature threw the one with the bumps into that tube."

Doctor Koi whipped her head around toward Xavier.

"That's not good."

More flicking antennas, tapping of Coco's legs and flailing of arms.

Doctor Koi whispered, "They're getting impatient."

"Just keep going," Xavier said.

"The female whatever is still alive but it's starting to look…"

"I don't understand. Try saying that another way, Don."

Don closed his eyes, made a smile emoji and with another arm, appeared to pat and rub where a tummy would be.

"Are you saying 'delicious'? That this female creature is starting to look delicious to the termants?"

Don's right arm flicked, *Yes.*

"Damn," said Doctor Koi. "Oh, dear. But after the last… They agreed not to… Oh dear. See, they captured a human a few years ago and… uh… Something must be going on. Their queen is very honest and upright. Has kept her word ever since that unfortunate incident. Oh dear."

Antennas waved. Coco tapped. Don translated.

"OK. That second creature has been drilling in that cave. Drilling?"

Flicks, taps and flails replied with an affirmative to Doctor Koi's question.

"The female saw the creature doing that. Tried to stop it from drilling. The drilling creature… The termants say it's male because it opens its skin where its legs meet and it shoots out a stream of liquid that smells like… Uh… Oh. That word is *ammonia*. They said his territory-marking stream—and they are some pissed off about that, no pun intended—smells like ammonia and they don't like that substance being anywhere near their nest." Doctor Koi's hand went to her mouth as she glanced over at Xavier. "The male pushed the female down into the cave. One of her limbs and perhaps her neck, too, are badly hurt so she can't climb out. They like her for trying to stop him, and that's why they didn't feed her to the nymphs yet."

Maureen gasped and her eyes traveled from one surfboard, cheerleader-pompomed creature to another. The one with the bear-trap jaws remained in the background, the tiny black beads of its eyes glittering in the overhead light.

"They don't want him drilling in there for two reasons. Their nest is close to there and surrounding their nest is a… I think she is calling it a metal. A metallic substance? She says it's…"

Don paused.

Doctor Koi waited.

Don made a signal.

"That means it's going to be a number."

Don flipped and flailed and flipped again.

"Is it ninety-two?"

Right arm, *Yes.*

"What's that? What's ninety-two?"

Don turned orange and his arms "exploded" outwards.

"Uranium," said Tovy. "Somebody's drilling near a uranium deposit." He climbed down from the step ladder and turned to face the termants. "We'll take care of this. Tell Queen we're on it."

A flailing and flickering of antennas, legs and arms.

From behind the group, the bear-trap jaws opened again to emit a snarl.

"Stop that," ordered Maureen. "We're going to help you."

In an instant, Bear-Trap was heading for Maureen but quicker than lightning, Coco was there between it and Maureen, to protect her.

Coco tapped.

Bear-Trap flicked its antennas and tapped twice with one leg.

Coco tapped again.

More flicks from Bear-Trap's antennas.

Don's arms flailed.

"The termant is insisting they be allowed to keep the damaged female for the nymphs to eat."

Coco stretched up higher to loom over Bear-Trap.

Bear-Trap's antennas reacted.

Coco tapped again but this time on Bear-Trap's head, between its antennas.

The bear-trap jaws shot out and snatched Coco, in one swift bite, into itself. It was as though a vacuum cleaner had just sucked up a fluff of under-the-bed dust.

Thuck.

Coco was gone.

But Don was there, too. Glowing red, his arms encircled Bear-Trap and *SNAP!* Bear-Trap was in two pieces and Coco—still in *one* piece—lay there on the floor between the broken Bear-Trap.

Two of the closest termants grabbed the pieces of Bear-Trap and with a flutter of pink frills and quivering antennas, led the rest of their cheerleaders' pompom-bearing surfboard allies toward the patio to disappear up the outside of the overhang.

"We haven't heard the last from them," said Xavier, almost forcing Maureen down onto the floor beside Coco. "Not by a long shot. We have to find that entry port on the Surface and stop that guy, whoever he is. But first, you have to help Coco."

"There you go with the orders again," said Maureen. "But this time, I... Oh, but... I don't know if I can do this or not. It's a spider, for God's sake. I have to actually touch a spider?"

She shivered, then bent down to look more closely at an inert Coco but as she did so, Coco twitched.

"OH! DEAR FUCKING LORD ABOVE. IT MOVED!"

Behind Maureen, Xavier and Doctor Koi leaned over her from their standing positions.

"Is she going to be OK?" asked Doctor Koi. "Maybe she's just in shock. She was in and out quick."

"Oh, no," said Maureen, reaching out a tentative hand to touch the fuzzy bag on Coco. "I think this underneath part was damaged. Is this the abdomen?"

"Uh. No," said Doctor Koi. "That's her… That's her egg sac."

"She has a baby spider in there?"

"Uh. No. More like a thousand. And it looks like they're on their way out."

"Shit."

25

"OK," SAID MAUREEN. "This leg looks broken. Maybe some duct tape? That should do it but oh, dear lord above, can you do anything about these things? Uck."

The fuzzy ping-pong-ball-sized spiderlings, dozens, milled around among Coco's legs, her body, and Maureen's knees. "If they touch me, I'll scream. I won't be able to help myself."

"They probably won't," said Xavier. "Their instinct is to get into their nursery nest. And they're aware that Mommy is the one who provides that for them. She'll be the one they go for."

Weakly, Coco tapped.

Don flailed, Doctor Koi translated. "'Yes. A nest. Never mind me. Take care of the children. They need a nest. I'll try...'"

From Coco's rear end came a thread.

Doctor Koi took hold of the end of it. "Whatever you do, do not pull on this or you'll rip her guts out."

"Oh, God, that's a pleasant thought!"

"Oh. There we go. We've got almost half a meter to work with already. Do you know how to knit?"

"What self-respecting woman my age doesn't? You have knitting needles?"

"Use your fingers."

"My fingers. I'm going to wrap that stuff around my fingers? Bad enough I have to touch it at all."

"Like this. See?" With the end of the thread coming out of Coco's rear end, Doctor Koi tied a loop around her left index finger. She pulled slightly and gently, looped then looped then looped until she had about fourteen loops. "See?" She plucked at the thread to undo the loops and handed the thread, knotted end first, to Maureen. "There you go."

Squeamishly, Maureen repeated the steps Doctor Koi had shown her, then worked her way back along the row, using her other index finger as the second makeshift knitting needle. "Hey, there we go. Row one done already. I thought this stuff was supposed to be sticky."

"That's only for spiders who use webs to catch their food."

"Oh, wait. Um. I think I need to do this extra loose." Maureen undid the row, re-looped it loosely, re-knit, slipped the completed row from her right hand's finger to the left one's, switching it the opposite way as she did so, to have the thread on the right. "We're going to have to go with the plain ol' garter stitch, I'm afraid. She doesn't do that? Use webs to catch her food?"

"She hunts."

"Oh. Not in packs though, eh?"

"Not as far as we know." Once again, the smile in Doctor Koi's eyes could not be hidden by merely covering the smile on her lips.

Within moments, because of the large loops, Maureen had nearly a foot square of web-nest.

Taps from Coco. Weak, but determined taps.

"Oh. She wants you to end that section. What's that, Don? Repeat that, please?"

Taps.

Flails.

"She's saying, 'Would you mind if I gave you specific directions at this point?'"

"Not at all. No. What do you want me to do?"

"'Tie that off. Don't break the thread. Set that section on the floor and draw out a string about the length of...'" Coco turned to look more closely at Maureen's hands.

"I only have two hands," said Maureen.

"'So you have. Sorry. Doctor Koi can be one of her extra hands. Stick that thread onto the floor right there.'"

Doctor Koi did as instructed.

"'Maureen needs to stretch that thread up about the length of her wrist to her elbow. Yes. Like that. Hey. She's good at that.'"

"Yeah? Maybe I was a spider in a former life."

"'Huh?'"

"Never mind."

"'Now start another web the same size. That's interesting what you're doing. You call it 'knitting'? Interesting. When I'm feeling better, you'll have to show me how to do that.'"

Maureen's laugh was not mocking, it was a laugh of relief and pure enjoyment from having made a new friend. Foreign as her new friend was, at least.

As Maureen knitted, the spiderlings came closer and closer to her. Some of them were already snuggling into the section laying on the floor. One or two were on Maureen's knee, reaching up for the bottom of the section she was working on.

"You all right with those little guys being so close to you?" asked Tovy who was adjusting the repaired draperies at floor level. "You're not going to freak out or anything, are you? Like jump up and squish any of them?"

"I think I have managed—by some miracle—to get over my spider phobia. I have no idea how I did it, but I think I did. They're kinda cute, actually."

"Um. We have company again," Tovy called out.

Down from the patio's overhang, several pompomed surfboards crawled into Doctor Koi's apartment along the wall. The only sounds were the whispered cursings of Maureen as she rose to her feet, dropping her knitting in the process. The two spiderlings who'd been hanging from the bottom of that section, scurried over to Coco.

The surfboards moved hither and thither, halting, twitching ahead, then sideways, before they shifted to the floor. A scratch on the side of one of them and a dark patch on the center back of another, said they were the same group that had been there earlier. But among them this time, in their center, a jewel in the crown they'd formed, sat another. One three times the size of any one of them.

"Greetings, Queen," said Doctor Koi, bowing her head.

"Greetings, Queen," echoed Xavier who then whispered to Maureen. "Bow your head to her."

Maureen complied without lowering her eyes from the huge antenna-waving surfboard creature.

A high-pitched hum filled the room.

Moaning, Maureen raised her hands to her ears.

A movement to the right. Bear-Trap came forward. On its back was a dark-brown, leather, purse-like object. The area where Bear-Trap had been split open was now a mere crack with a thin line of dark, congealed honey along it. Bear-Trap's movements were steady, determined. It stopped in front of Coco.

The hum ceased.

"That wail is something else. Sheesh."

"Hush," cautioned Xavier. "And have some respect. She just lost her husband."

Maureen laughed.

"Stop. I'm serious. Have some respect. Her husband passed away a few days ago. And he was a lot better with communications than she is. Believe me! Quiet. We have to make sure we don't mis-read anything."

Doctor Koi spoke to Maureen's frown. "A queen and king mate for life. Even on the Surface, termite queens can live for thirty, forty, even fifty years. The bond they form would obviously be a strong one."

"No kidding."

"Hush. Shut up for once and listen."

"Queen is also nearing the end of *her* life. She is, from what we can figure, probably close to sixty years of age."

"And that presents a *big* problem," Xavier added.

26

THE ONE THEY had called Queen, motioned with her front legs to Bear-Trap.

Bear-Trap moved even closer to Coco.

"Hey, hey, now," said Maureen, taking a protective step toward her new arachnid friend. "Don't you be doing anything to her again or I'll be the one snapping you in half."

Both Xavier and Doctor Koi jumped in to pull Maureen back.

"Look at him," Maureen growled. "He's practically on top of her. You know what happened before. She hasn't even recovered from that episode. Asshole."

"It's not a he, it's a she, but only sort of a she so we call those ones, *its*."

"Honest to God, you guys."

Bear-Trap moved even closer to Coco.

Coco, holding her damaged leg underneath her, rose shakily to her feet. Using a rear leg, she managed to kick what so far existed of the knitted, all-important web-nest backwards, toward Maureen.

Maureen shuffled just enough to have the web-nest between and slightly behind her feet.

Bear-Trap appeared to bow with its rear two legs keeping its back end up. With a middle leg, it slid the "purse" from its back and laid this on the floor in front of Coco. Rising again to its normal level, and using two front legs, it slowly pulled open the purse and turned it upside down.

From it, poured hundreds of spiderlings. Coco's undamaged legs tapped and skittered among her young as they rushed toward her, below her, then into the partially built web-nest Maureen was guarding.

"Gawd!" Maureen stood her ground as the fuzzy, eight-legged ping pong balls gathered around her feet. A forced smile formed as she asked, "What's that purse thing made of? It's lovely."

"Changing the subject there, dear girl?"

"Don't forget, I'm just now, as of only hours ago, getting over a spider phobia that has dogged me since childhood."

"You've got this."

"Don't say that. Don't ever use that expression around me. You have no idea what's going on inside my head. I don't think I've got this in the least way possible. I'm trying to distract myself by thinking, since we have a textile manufacturer…"

Coco raised a leg at her and twitched that foot.

"… we might consider a purse—maybe even a shoe—maker." Maureen's laugh came across as even more forced than her smile had been. "I could go out in style."

The hum began again.

It was coming from Queen.

Maureen covered her ears and squeezed her eyes shut so missed the quick motion of Bear-Trap toward the duct tape on Coco's leg. But she heard the snap as the duct tape was cut and removed.

Snap. It was gone. Then consumed.

"What are you doing, you idiot?"

Two cheerleader surfboard creatures were instantly there, flipping Coco onto the floor, making Maureen struggle in the arms of both Xavier and Doctor Koi.

But one of the cheerleader surfboards was helping Bear-Trap hold the broken pieces of Coco's leg together.

Maureen stopped struggling.

The second cheerleader surfboard rose to its hind legs, then dropped down and vomited onto Coco's leg. A flurry of the front legs of all three termants soon had the vomited honey spread over the damaged area. Within what seemed like mere seconds, the leg was completely healed with only the tiniest line of honey oozing through the now almost-invisible crack.

Coco was instantly on all eights to dash between Maureen's feet from where she snatched the knitted web-nest away to run toward the patio. And like a tsunami of fuzzy, brown, cat-toy balls, hundreds of baby spiders followed her.

Xavier, still protectively right beside Maureen, and grinning, reached up. "Ah. There's one in your hair."

He made a grab for it, but Maureen was faster and she tucked it into her cupped hand and raced to the patio where Coco was placing the web-nest in the corner behind a chair.

"Here's another one." She placed it into the nest where Coco was fussing with strings of web. "Want some help with that?"

Don was just then crawling out of the water and his arm signals indicated to Maureen that he'd done this before, so Maureen stepped back.

As Don's last arm rose onto the patio, water came with it, and this caused several of the spiderlings to flow into it past him into the sea behind him.

Maureen called out, "Oh, no. Some of them fell in."

Tovy's head appeared from behind the draperies. "Don't worry. They weigh next to nothing. Takes over a hundred of them to weigh a gram. They won't sink. Their feet hold them up."

"Wow."

"That's how they attract their food. Their feet from below appear to be bugs or something. That draws the fish. And nom, nom, nom."

"Well I don't like the idea of fish swimming around below those cute little darlings maybe thinking *they*'re food."

By now, Don was back in the water with two of his arms forming a moving, gradually enclosing corral of sorts as he helped Coco herd the little ones back onto the patio. Successful, he flailed his arms at Maureen and Coco.

"He says he can keep an eye on the kids while you guys go back inside and talk to Queen."

Don flailed again and formed a laugh emoji.

"He says he can watch *them* with one eye and *you* with the other."

"Can he really do that?"

"That, he can."

"Octopuses are creepy," said Maureen.

Don twirled and flapped his arms.

"What did he say?"

Tovy, smiling, said, "*That*, I will *not* translate."

"She's waiting for you," said Xavier, once more drawing Maureen in close to himself. "She has something to tell us all."

Translations began again with Doctor Koi doing the speaking parts.

"There's a group of young upstarts who are recently aware that there is tasty food at the Surface and they've been working their way around and up, trying to locate how to get to the Surface to capture that tasty food. That's how they found out about the male drilling. And the dying female. Queen is both pleased and displeased."

"And that means…?"

"She is pleased they are hunting for this food—"

A gasp from Maureen, then, "Hunting?" made the tiny black eyes of all eight cheerleader surfboards plus Queen's focus on her.

Maureen's own eyes glanced up at Xavier who shot back I-told-you-so eyebrows along with a shrug. His lips said, "Silence."

Doctor Koi continued. "She is pleased they are hunting for food, but displeased that they are doing it on the Surface. There aren't many of them know about the Surface and they want to keep it that—"

A single twitch of a single antenna from Queen.

"Queen and *a few chosen termants* are the only ones who are and should be aware of the Surface." Doctor Koi bowed her head to Queen. "My apologies, Queen."

A tap from Queen.

"Those young ones were not among the chosen so, of course, had to be disposed of. And were. Just now."

Maureen's mouth formed the beginning of the word *What?* but she closed it before anything exited.

"Good girl," muttered Xavier from the side of his mouth. "See? You can do it. Keep it up. Keep it shut."

"Because Queen is nearing the end of her days, it's critically important that the… Oh, now she's using the word human." Doctor Koi turned to Xavier and Maureen to say, "That puts the onus on us."

Xavier leaned down to speak quietly to Maureen. "She's offering us an ultimatum. We take care of the problem, or she'll handle it her way."

"The male human must be stopped from drilling into the nest. There are new queens being developed there. It will mean the end of her 'clan' if the nymphs are destroyed. There's another clan… Uh. For want of a better expression I'll translate as 'down here' and they live…" Doctor Koi pointed in the direction of the far end of the cavern. "… kilometers away in that direction. They are a different clan, she says. Very different." Doctor Koi spoke softly to Maureen. "I don't think they like each other." Then she went back to translating. "Like the Queen's clan, they rob graves, but would, of course, prefer live humans if they ever had a chance to taste one of you people."

Queen's eyes moved away from Maureen's face to nowhere in particular.

Almost in unison, the other cheerleader pompomed creatures did the same.

Queen flicked her antennas at Doctor Koi.

Doctor Koi translated. "'We don't want that, do we?'"

Queen's eyes flicked momentarily at Maureen's, but only momentarily.

"Years ago, a truce formed between the clans, but there has recently been the occasional skirmish. 'We don't go to their territory and they don't come to ours. Except…'"

Queen's eyes were on Maureen's again, then away.

"'Except when our young upstarts—and theirs—get stupid ideas into their heads and begin to cause problems. Like snooping around on the Surface or into each other's territory. So we have to interv—'"

Queen's hum, although brief, made Maureen cringe. Then Queen waved her antennas back and forth like they were over-crossing windshield wipers.

"Oh. You don't want me to translate that?"

Queen's eyes went to Xavier's, to Maureen, to Xavier's.

"She can be trusted."

Queen's eyes bore into Xavier's.

"She can. I promise."

"I thought you never made promises," whispered Maureen.

"Shut up."

Doctor Koi continued. "A small group of their young ones broke protocol and entered the territory here not too long ago. They spotted the humans here… And…"

Queen flicked her front leg.

"They discovered all of us here. Me, Xavier, Tovy and Rocky, and killed and ate… They ate somebody before we could stop them. Somebody who used to live here with us."

Maureen's face collapsed into a frown of compassion.

"We had no choice. And I'm speaking of we as myself and Xavier and Tovy and Rocky… We had no choice but to… but to kill these young ones. Queen knew. She helped us dispose of what you might call the evidence. But if members of that clan ever find out what we did… Or even worse, if they ever learn there are humans down here. Live food and not what they get as roadkill or from cemeteries…"

Queen tapped and flicked. Coco tapped and flicked. Don flailed.

Doctor Koi bowed her head again. "My apologies. I digressed. 'The other clan—and there are more than one but this one is the closest to us, so the most dangerous—would surely take over the lava tubes, kill all the termants and eggs here, and eventually find the Surface where they will begin to capture and consume humans. They will feed humans to their nymphs. The population will explode. They'll take over the entire surface of the planet.'

"Queen and her people have been keeping an extra eye out for them so that's why those young folks decided to go to the surface, even though that is absolutely FORBIDDEN. They were just trying to help.

"Queen had a— Do you really want me to say it like that?"

Queen tapped.

Doctor Koi continued. "She had 'a little talk' with the young ones about what would happen if one of them happened to be seen by someone. But they disobeyed her yet again. They made the wrong choice even though it worked out well that they discovered the… the male human digging into our world."

"And that," whispered Xavier, "is why we haven't explored past this cavern. It's in case more of those other ones find out about us. Or more of the young ones in the clan."

"Why don't you just leave? Like, mind your own business kind of thing?"

Xavier squeezed Maureen closer to himself. "There are places we don't want to go with you yet. And I'm not talking physical places."

Doctor Koi obviously had not heard this exchange between Maureen and Xavier, nor had Queen, it seemed. Doctor Koi continued to translate. "Queen admits that they, too, take an occasional human but usually one that is only recently deceased. They like the older ones because they're chewy."

"What?"

Xavier said, "OK. Chewy-er. Humans are chewy to start with but get better with age."

"At least we're good for something, eh?"

Doctor Koi resumed. "This helps develop the jaws of both the workers and the warriors. The woman who was pushed is at the perfect stage for consumption by the upcoming nymphs who will develop into new queens. That's why she's so tempting. It doesn't matter, male or female, although they do prefer female. The only problem with this female is that she is one of our group so she's been consum—"

"Whoa, whoa," said Xavier. "I'll handle this little issue later? OK?"

"Oh. Right," said Doctor Koi, whose eyes jumped over to Maureen then back to Xavier.

Queen's eyes also flicked to and away from Maureen and back again, but this time to her body.

"They must be alive for queen nymphs to develop. If they can keep one alive after that, it's a bonus for everyone."

Queen flicked and tapped. This time, the other cheerleader surfboards reacted to what she said by tap-dancing on all six feet and swaying their antennas back and forth.

"That indicates laughter," Xavier explained.

"What did she say that's so funny?"

Doctor Koi wasn't smiling. "She said, 'We all like a wee snack of raw meat once in a while, don't we?'"

"What? Ew!"

"That's it," said Xavier. "You, dear girl, are out of here."

Maureen's protests were for naught.

27

"SO WHY DO you have all this room," Maureen swept her hand from painted partition to painted partition in Xavier's quarters. "… and everybody else gets only a cave?"

"This area doubles as… uh…"

"As uh. What's an uh?"

"Triples, I guess you could say."

"As what? Come on, Xavier. Out with it. Tell me what's really going on."

"Let me put these dishes in the washer first."

"I'll help you—"

"Sit. It'll take me two seconds. Want your tea warmed up?"

"You're driving me crazy."

Xavier laughed. "There are times I might like to hear that expression coming from a woman, but today isn't one of them. Be right back." He disappeared behind one of the partitions.

Maureen crossed her arms and leaned back in her chair. She shook her head. "Honest to God, that guy is…"

"There. Done. Now. Where were we?" Xavier moved his chair around to the side of the table from its original across-from-her position.

"Is this where the term, to make a move on someone came from?" Maureen asked this without emotion in either her voice or on her face.

"Think back. Think back to when you were helping Don and Paulo after they were attacked."

Maureen relaxed her arms and leaned slightly forward. "OK."

"You were handling honey. Right?"

"Yeah." She shrugged. "Tovy had some. So does Doctor Koi. I used it on Don. On Paulo, too."

"Concentrate. This is extremely important."

Her head made a sideways bobble. "OK. So?"

"Did you at any time touch the honey with your fingers or did it get on any part of you? Your actual flesh, I mean."

Maureen laughed. "What? This is stupid."

"And most importantly, did you happen to, if you did get any of it on your fingers, did you happen to lick your finger or anything?"

"Now you're creeping me out. What the fuck are you talking about?"

"Did you get any of it on you?"

"No. I'm a trained nurse. I know how to avoid touching bodily fluids that are oozing out of victims."

"I'm not talking about what was coming out of Don or Paulo, I'm talking about the honey. Just the honey. You tied strips of cloth around both of them, right?"

"Yes. What? Am I in court now? Am I going to be sued?"

"Bondye mwen, ou anbete mwen!"

"What'd you say?"

"Roughly translated? My God, you can be annoying."

Maureen tsked. "Sorreee."

"Did you at any time physically touch or consume any of that honey?"

"I don't think so."

Xavier's head dropped. "She doesn't think so." He adjusted his chair to be able to look more directly at her. "If you touched the honey with your finger or with any part of your body, you will probably be fine. But if you happened to accidentally or unconsciously touch that finger or wipe the honey off that body part or clothing, and consume even a molecule of it, you are in deep, deep, deep trouble."

Maureen lowered one eyebrow and raised the other at Xavier. "That is about the dumbest thing I've ever heard. Honey is antibacterial. It's healthy. It heals. It—"

"Bee honey. Surface bee honey. Yes. It's harmless, healthy and doesn't rot, not even over thousands of years, but I'm not talking about bee honey. I'm not talking about Surface honey. What we have here is termant honey."

"Termant honey. Is there something poisonous in it?"

"Just the opposite."

Maureen's chuckle was cut short by the expression on Xavier's face. "What's so bad about being the opposite to poison?"

"Remember that old movie Shangri-La?"

"It was *about* Shangri-La, it was called Lost Horizon." She patted his knee. "It's OK, dear boy. I always used to get it mixed up, too."

"I stand corrected, *dear girl*. Either way, the people there couldn't leave for any period of time without aging to the point they should be. Like two hundred years old, some of them."

"It's one of my faves. I think the best scene was when she was gasping for breath outside there on the mountain with him, and her face was going all wrinkly. They did a super job of the special effects for that scene. I wonder how they managed to do that without CGI."

"Maureen…"

"Shit. Wait. Are you telling me…?"

"I am. We have all consumed their honey. Their honey is what healed us. It's what has been regenerating us for years. It keeps us alive and well. It keeps those who live Topside alive and well. The price one pays, *dwa*? The termants insisted that we all take it orally." To himself, Xavier muttered. "How naïve can one be?" Then again to Maureen, "That way, anyone who knew about them would soon die if they went to the Surface. And that's another reason they don't want their own… How can I explain this? Their own 'people.' They don't want their own people up on the Surface, either. In case they have an issue, shall we say, and begin to deteriorate, get stuck up there and are discovered. Everything down here is fed that honey. Everything. The termants are essentially drug lords. To them, it's just 'business' so they don't think anything's wrong with that. Their reward is not monetary, of course. It's… It's to maintain… To maintain their entire world. Hard to get into your head that keeping a person alive is actually putting him in shackles, isn't it?"

"Flabbergast me any further and I'm liable to need some of that shit because you're going to give me a heart attack."

"All of us, down here and Topside, were at one time addicted to street drugs or booze."

"And now you're addicted to their honey."

"It's not addictive. Not in the least. We just can't continue to exist without consuming it."

"You have to keep taking it?"

"The more time we spend on the Surface, the more we become… I guess 'depleted' would be the best way to describe it."

"Damn. Is there anything you can do?"

"Nothing. We've spent years trying to figure it out but we can't. Now may I get back to my original question?"

"I know enough not to lick my fingers after I tend to a patient. So no. I did not consume any of that stuff. But what if I got it on my hands or something?"

"Let me see." Xavier laid the back of his own hands on the table and flicked his fingers inward.

Maureen laid her hands in his. "What are you looking for?"

"Any sign of reduced wrinkling or lack of age spots."

"And?"

Xavier flipped her hands over. "Nope. You're OK. They look exactly the way an extremely elderly lady's hands should look."

He laughed.

Maureen didn't.

"To be perfectly honest with you, I don't blame them for doing this to us."

"You'd better expand on that one."

And expand, Xavier did.

Without the termants, the underground sea would die. There would be no water or oxygen to breathe in by some species who would then breathe out carbon dioxide for those plants that were "down below." Those plants that the creatures down below consumed—plus each other. "The creature who attacked Don and Paulo probably does consume plants," said Xavier, "But it obviously prefers a wee snack of raw meat now and again, too."

"Gotcha so far," said Maureen. "But plants need light, don't they? And there's no sunlight down here. But it's bright. How does that happen?"

"You'd have to ask Doctor Koi about that. I'm not an expert. All I know is that it's not only those clusterwinks who provide light. There are lots of other species that glow. Don't ask me to name them. Please." Xavier held his hands up, palms toward Maureen. "I know there's a microscopic one that essentially coats everything, even the lava tubes. Remember that weird light you and Sandra were freaking out about?" He pointed to the ceiling. "The termants have made some kind of agreement, I guess you could call it, to get them to act as automatic lighting systems in our apartments, too. They turn off when we go to sleep and…"

"They watch us?"

"Sorry to say, dear girl, that they do." A teasing smile touched the corner of Xavier's mouth.

"So we can't really get away with anything then, can we?"

"I'm just teasing. They're microscopic. They don't have eyes or ears or anything." He leaned in toward Maureen, widened his eyes, emitted his teasing evil laugh and said, "At least, I don't think so."

"Oh stop it."

Laughing normally, he leaned back again. "We can 'turn them off' by a switch. I don't know how it works. None of us does. There's an elaborate what you might call 'electrical system' throughout this entire world but it's not exactly electricity as we know it. Same with their what we call radio frequencies on the Surface. Cell phones can't communicate through solid rock. What they have down here can. Tovy says it's something like neutrinos—"

"Oh. Sandra told me about those things. They're shooting around everywhere and through everything, like billions of them at a time?"

"It's not those, just something like them. We don't know. Tovy has no clue. We're just happy we can communicate and don't care how."

"What you were saying before is true then," said Maureen. "It's not just the gold and the gems we have to keep hidden. If people on the Surface learn about the healing properties of that special termant honey, Big Pharma will find a way to 'create' it so they can hold the patent and control it. And if people on the Surface find out about the electrical system down here and the special WiFi that can go through solid rock, that means they'll want it for themselves. That means they'll kill everything down here who provide all that for free. That means they'll totally annihilate this entire world. It's not the first time humans have done that kind of thing."

"Indeed."

"So that's why you're going along with what that queen termant wants."

"Like I said, we have no choice."

"I think I agree with your compassion. But only about eighty percent just yet. But wait. Are you telling me that the termants somehow can produce oxygen? Enough to keep us going down here?"

"I don't know how it works. You'd have to ask Rocky or maybe Tovy. But when they chew at the rocks and eat them, they convert the stuff in the rocks into all manner of science-y things. All I know is, Surface termites eat wood. Our guys eat rock and more or less fart oxygen and other elements that form the basis of the necessities of life."

"No shit!"

"Shit, too, I suppose. But the farts are the more valuable."

Both Maureen and Xavier laughed.

28

MAUREEN AND XAVIER were about to head over to Doctor Koi's apartment to see if anyone had heard any more news about anything. Especially if there had been any more breaches: either into or out of the underground sea.

"I understand now why it's so important that we find out who told those guys how to get down here. And about the zombie powder. Sorry for being such a pain."

"I knew you were a quick learner, dear girl." He turned her to face him directly then placed his hands on her upper arms. "And as sad as it makes me to know you'll be leaving us, it makes me happy that you won't be forced to stay here."

Without comment or facial expression, she pulled away from him.

"You were asking how we got here in the first place."

Maureen made no comment or reaction to show she had heard him.

"I was the first one here."

Maureen appeared to be examining the paintings on the closest partition, but her mind was obviously focused elsewhere.

"I was a drunk and a druggie but a secret one as I was trying my best to maintain the illusion that I was a respectable Vodou Master. Priest. I already had a couple of... I almost said 'customers.' How television evangelist of me, *dwa*? One of them was Vainy, by the way.

"All I needed was a church. Or the facsimile of one. I was walking along... Actually, right along the street where you live. And I, literally, fell into the exact same underground tunnel you and your friend discovered. The tunnel was right there. It had been built by humans ages ago. Business people wanting a quick, easy and safe way to transport alcoholic beverages, I think it was. Something in my alcohol- and drug-fuddled mind was telling me that there could be a stash of undiscovered wine or whisky in that tunnel, so off I went exploring. Do you want to sit down?"

"Is it going to be that bad?"

"No. I promise. I think you've already heard the worst."

"I'm fine standing. Thanks for asking. Oh. Or is that an excuse for you to be able to set *your* old bum down? You tired? Dear boy?"

"I have my honey to keep me going, remember?"

"Is that supposed to be funny?"

"I guess not. Anyway, I was wandering around down in that tunnel. They've since closed off the hole I fell into, by the way."

"Who has? The termants?"

"The City. They don't like getting sued when folks twist an ankle or something."

No response from Maureen.

"So there I was, wandering around and I saw this stick jutting out from a slit in the tunnel wall. It was wiggling and there was a moan or wail coming from inside the rocks there. You following me?"

"I am."

"So the doctor in me, the do-no-harm guy, the treat-the-ill man, had to examine it. There was a tiny foot at the end of this stick. It was an animal of some sort."

"How big was this stick thing?"

Xavier held out his bent arm. "I'd say from my wrist to my elbow. Skinny, though. The foot was about the size of a kitten's foot, but the toes were as long as your fingers. Three toes."

"Three." Maureen laughed. "And in your alcohol- and drug-induced stupor you figured it was E.T.?"

Xavier threw his head back and laughed. "Probably."

"Then what?"

"I got myself up onto the street again, snapped a narrow branch—actually two—off a tree and went back down and pried open the slit the stick was sticking out of."

"And?"

"And that's when I decided to go off booze and drugs forever."

Maureen smiled. "That weird, was it?"

"That weird. Yes. Those guys, the termants, have been smoothing out the lava tubes for thousands of years. I'd bet hundreds of thousands of years. They're the ones who built the elevators."

"Wow."

"One of the Warriors attacked me. Bit my arm." He held out his arm and pointed to an area close to his elbow. "But, of course, there's no scar anymore. One of the Neutrals stopped it from causing further damage. Another one puked on me.

"Even in my drunken and drugged state, I knew that what was going on was going on for real and not just in my head. I had to go through withdrawal, of course, but I've never touched the stuff again and never had the slightest desire to do so since. But every time I go to the Surface, I'm depleted. So now it's the honey. I don't have the slightest desire for honey, but I have to take it.

"Saving that one single termant is what saved my own life. In many ways. They wouldn't have actually killed me, they would have..." He tossed an insincere smile in Maureen's direction. "Let's not go there just yet, OK?"

"I'm glad they didn't kill you."

Again, Xavier turned Maureen to face him full on. He pulled her in close to his body. "So am I."

Two beeps from Xavier's pocket ended that conversation, and any further developments.

29

"**AH. WE WERE** wondering where you guys had disappeared to," called Tovy from the patio. "These little guys are absolutely adorable. Too bad they have to grow up and move away."

"Where do they move to?" asked Maureen.

"Who knows," Doctor Koi said. "But if you're worried about them, don't be. They aren't on the termants' menu. No matter what the clan. Nor are we on theirs. What's up, Xavier? You look worried."

"I've just been trying to explain to Maureen about the …" He turned his head this way and that, wall to wall and floor to ceiling to floor again. "Any of them around?"

A snort from Tovy on the patio. "Are they ever *not* around?"

"… the dangers of consuming their honey. By the way, our, uh, 'visitors' have come out of their dream world. I think it's time to start the interviews." To Maureen he said, "You ready to tackle this?"

Maureen nodded and sat on the sofa in the TV room from where she glanced from corner to corner. "This room will be good. It will set them at ease. If we had a lamp swinging above us or we were slapping our palms with a cop baton, we wouldn't be able to get their trust."

"Ya think?" laughed Tovy, still out on the patio. "Where's Rocky anyway? Shouldn't he be here?"

"He's Topside," said Doctor Koi. "Spent the night there. He'll connect with Officer Bob when *their* interviewee becomes available."

Maureen rose to her feet. "Topside's OK for you guys to be?"

"Topside's fine. It is a sublevel, right?"

"Uh. Sure. Whatever you say."

"I can explain in elemental terms, if you like," called out Tovy. "Literal elemental terms."

"I'll pass."

Xavier asked, "What do you need us to do?"

"Move this chair over to that corner. That'll be yours. He'll see you over to the side. You'll be watching his facial expressions to figure out if he's telling the truth or not."

"I'm no good at that."

"Do you lie to everybody, Doctor Xavier? Honest to God. Does he do that to you guys, too?"

Doctor Koi's laughing eyes met Maureen's as a *harumph* came from the patio.

"And put that chair directly across from the sofa where I'll be sitting. Right in the middle. That will give me a somewhat pompous edge. Yes?"

Xavier smiled at Doctor Koi. "She's something else, isn't she?"

Maureen ignored his comment. "And since we won't be handcuffing them to that coffee table…" Maureen threw a smile at Xavier. "You can move that out of the way."

A nod from Xavier asked Doctor Koi to help him slide the coffee table out of the way.

"That's perfect. They'll feel more exposed that way."

"Ah. Good plan. But before we go collect them—"

"Not 'them.' One at a time."

"Up to you, uh, 'Detective Maureen,' but I should tell you something else…"

Maureen's hand went to her chin and its index finger tapped. "Let's start with the one who isn't that young woman's ex."

"That makes sense," said Doctor Koi. "What were you going to say, Xavier?"

"I was going to fill Maureen in on a little more information about the man I suspect is behind this."

"Is this going to be gross, too?" Maureen asked.

Xavier shook his head. "Vainy befriended me. Years ago."

"Oh, *that* guy. You said he became one of your church members or something?"

"Yes. *That* guy. At first, I thought it was because he was actually interested in my culture, my spiritual beliefs, you know? And he was so eager to help. As I think back, he was actually insistent, saying he wanted desperately to help counsel people." Xavier's laugh was quiet and without humor. "Counsel people? More like bring them under his control by extracting as much information out of them as possible.

"This would be one of the ways to eliminate me from what I had started setting up in this bizarre world of ours. It's not only those on the Surface who don't know what goes on down here, nobody Topside knows either. Nobody but Missus Cheffie, and now Stan, know what goes on Seaside.

"I think Vainy also became jealous of my status. It wasn't just the controlling of our people thing. I mean, there I was, taking homeless drug-addicted elderly people off the streets and setting them up in a comfortable home with everything and anything they could ever desire. I helped them get over their addictions and with a… With a little help from my dear friends the termants and…" Xavier's eyes roamed the room once again as he spoke more loudly, "… and especially their queen… I was able to heal them of any and all physical ills they might have had. Have you ever noticed the absence of homeless seniors on the streets of Ottawa, Maureen?"

"Come to think of it, there really aren't that many, are there?"

"That's because they're usually dead by the time they get to any significant age." Tovy's head disappeared beyond the draperies again as he bent over to address the spiderlings there. "Isn't that right, you long-legged little darlings?"

"Vainy was quick to notice that we seem to have an endless supply of funds. He has asked me about it numerous times while trying to make it look like he's not all that interested but… Hey. I'm not stupid when it comes to people who try to use me to get something. I spent many years on the street.

"Anyway. I suspect he is trying to get me out of the way so he can take over. I'm not certain if he knows about the valuable gems down here—"

"Diamonds and rubies and emeralds galore," said Tovy. "And gold. Tons of gold. Literal tons. If you want to learn how volcanoes produce those wondrous gifts, Maureen, I can tell you any time you want."

"But not right now," said Xavier. "Right now, the important thing on our menu is— Ack. Poor choice of words there, I guess. Menu? We uh… We can't have Surface people find out about this. Any of this."

"That's the last thing you guys would want," said Maureen. "The last thing I would want, too, now that I'm getting my head around what's going on."

"Yup," continued Tovy. "You let the Surface folks find out about down here and we're all screwed. All of us. Everything."

Nods all around.

"But how do you get away with converting the gold and gems into cash?" Maureen asked. "You don't just go into Loblaws and hand the cashier a gold nugget and ask for change, do you?”

“Our friend Officer Bob takes care of that,” Xavier said. “He knows a lot of… people. People who know how to convert that kind of thing into cash, offshore bank accounts and credit cards. And nothing's illegal. Clandestine, iffy, but legal. See, if the government finds out there's a stash of gold down here, they aren't going to like it.”

“Why not?”

“If the market gets flooded with gold, the market goes to hell.”

“Oh. Gotcha. Damn. No.” She laughed. “They wouldn't like that at all, would they? They'd start taxing us even worse than they are now.”

“They'd sent out the troops to find us. To shut this place down. In secret they'd keep it going, though. Economics is everything. Unfortunately.”

“And speaking of saving asses…” Tovy leaned up straight again to speak directly to the group. “If somebody's digging up there, if they happen to kill off the termant babies with a uranium explosion, bingo, there goes everything. What's going on right now is the development of a replacement for Queen. Something happens to her replacement? Bam. There goes an entire clan of termants. An entire civilization. Nothing could exist in this area anymore without them. Not to mention, all of us down here would die a rather quick and nasty death without oxygen. Or honey.”

“That's what Xavier was telling me. Scary. I don't even want to think about it.”

“You know… I'm not so sure Vainy's the one digging the tunnel,” said Xavier, scratching his head. “What if Billy's behind it? What if he's found out somehow that Pamela is living down here? I mean most everybody knows about the tunnels under Ottawa so maybe he heard something. Maybe he's thinking along those lines?”

“Could be,” said Doctor Koi. “But the only way we can find out is by asking. Yes? Let's go get them.”

30

IT WAS OBVIOUSLY no surprise to anyone that the man Xavier and Doctor Koi guided in was hung over to the extreme. Hands quivering, he sat in the indicated chair across from Maureen, who, as planned, was in the exact center of the sofa, playing royalty.

"My name is Maureen. I'm going to be uh… asking you some questions. Are you up for that?"

The man's bloodshot eyes looked out over their puffy pinkish-yellow lower lids with a message that said, *Are you out of your ever-loving mind?* "Andrew. Can I get a fookin' drink, um, ma'am? And I mean in the way of an alcoholic beverage? Coffee won't do nothin' for me. Least not yet. Jesus, Mary and Josephine. Oh, man."

"Right here, Andrew," said Xavier, offering a cup, sans saucer, and with the handle turned away from any trembling fingers or thumb. "This will fix you up pretty much instantly."

"What is it?"

"Just give it a try, Andrew. One sip should do it."

"Why should I trust *you*?"

"I'm a doctor."

"Oh." Andrew sipped. "What the fuck is this shit?"

"Medicine. I told you, I'm a doctor."

Maureen said, "Psst." And she waved Xavier over to bend so she could whisper in his ear. "Are you actually giving him some of that… that…? Isn't that a death sentence? Or is that what your plan is?"

"Not if he sticks around. We can't actually let him go, can we? He knows too much. He'll be fine. A few weeks in my digs and we won't have any more complaints from him. Ever."

"If you're going torture him, why do I have to do this phony interrogation?"

"Oh. Wow," said Andrew. "That's interesting." His chuckle was hoarse but real. "Wow. You sure you're not the Lady of Fatima or something, Doc? That's… Wow. Works faster than a shot o' hooch. Any day. It's a goddamn miracle. Tastes really grossly over-sweet, but damn, it worked. Wow. So like, uh, what do you want to know, Marie?"

"Maureen."

"Oh, yeah. OK. Sorry. So sorry. I'm Andrew. Hi."

"Hi Andrew. And you're forgiven. You can relax. Like I said, I'd like the answer to some questions. My first question is, do you know where you are?"

"Um." Andrew glanced around at the walls and floor of Doctor Koi's apartment. His eyes focused on the patio where Tovy still sat.

Tovy waved.

Off the edge of the patio was the top of Don's head and the horizontal slit of one eye. Andrew appeared not to notice. Perhaps, because of his heavy drinking habits, he was used to seeing things, so used to ignoring some of the things he saw, or those things he didn't want to see.

"I'd say I'm in some kind of underground cave by the sea but that would be absolutely ridiculous so I won't be saying that." He chuckled.

"But you'd be right, Andrew," said Maureen with nary a smile on either her lips or in her eyes. "Next question. How did you get here?"

"Oh. Uh. Lemme see. We went into a tunnel. Hey, did you know there are tunnels under the city? Like tunnels under Ottawa? Ottawa of all places? Boring, ordinary Ottawa. The city that fun forgot."

"I did."

"So… We went through this tunnel. But we had, like, a map, eh?"

"A map?"

"Yeah. Billy had it. Some dude gave it to him. And he didn't even have to ask. It was like the dude knew that Billy's looking for his wife."

"Don't you mean his ex-wife?"

"No, no. Everybody's saying that but she's not his ex, she's his wife-wife. She disappeared somewhere. Billy says she got kidnapped and this dude said he knows where they're keeping her. And he offered to help Billy. Said he's a… What did he call it? Some kind of religious guy… guru… hoodoo… Something like that. I can't remember."

"Priest? Minister? Evangelist?"

"No." Andrew shook his head. "Something else. I forget."

"Rabbi? Imam? Monk? Friar?"

"He didn't say it very loud. It was like it was a secret. But not a bad secret. It was like he was being really humble about it." Andrew's brow wrinkled. "I didn't actually hear it, I guess. He said it to Billy. Just Billy. Like real low. And Billy got all happy when he heard it. Said, 'That's totally cool, man. Come on, Andrew. She's down below. We can go find her and rescue her from the people who took her.'"

"And that's when he gave Billy the map?"

"Yeah."

"Do you remember the dude's name?"

"I think it's Italian. Not Mario or Tony or any of those regular ones. It was… Oh. Yeah. It started with a V. It was…"

Andrew closed his eyes and Maureen took the opportunity to glance over at Xavier, behind and to her left of the sofa, and to Doctor Koi, to the right and behind Andrew's chair.

Doctor Koi crossed her fingers.

"Vanni. The dude's name is Vanni."

"And that's all Vanni said? Just gave you guys the map and off you went?"

"Just like that and just as easy. But we never did find her. Not yet anyway. The map was gone when we woke up. I'm guessing you guys took it?" He winked at Xavier. "But we didn't need it anymore anyway. We got to where it ended. I guess here is there, eh?"

Xavier said, "I guess it is."

"He gave us each a bottle of rum. Said it would bring us luck because of the name of it. I prefer scotch if somebody's going to be giving me something for free, but it was really nice. Kind of spicy with off-tones of…" Andrew laughed. "… off-tones and hints of… shit, I don't know. Spice or something, I guess. Took a course in wine tasting maybe fifteen, twenty years ago, but any information—if it sunk in in the first place—is loooong gone!" He laughed again. "Never much liked wine. Not nearly enough of a kick to it, eh?"

"So you said the name of the rum would bring you luck. Care to share?"

"Sure. It was… Uh. I'm sorry. I can't remember. I'm sorry. You know what I would like right now though. Something to eat and a nap. Is that possible?"

"It most certainly is. Xavier will take you to his…"

"My clinic," said Xavier, rising from his chair. "We'll get you all settled in."

Without argument or complaint, Andrew accepted Xavier's hand on his upper arm as Xavier led him out of Doctor Koi's apartment.

☺

Within a short time, Xavier had returned with the other interviewee at his side. This man was shaking even more than Andrew had been. He was tall, skinny, with a belly bulge where his liver would be, and an orange tinge to his skin. His cigarette-smoke-yellow and gray hair was sticking up in clumps; for his apparent age, perhaps fifty, he hadn't lost much of it. Several days' worth of red beard covered his upper lip and jaw.

As directed, he sat.

"So," said Maureen, forcing a smile. "If you don't mind, I'd like to ask you some questions."

"Give me a DRINK."

"Your friend Andrew tells us that your wife has been kidnapped. I can't imagine how stressful that must be."

"I don't give a hoot in hell right now where anybody is or what they're doing, all I want is a shot of rum. A shot of anything."

"Andrew tells us you found your way here through the use of a map."

"Could I just get a drink?"

"Maybe later." She shrugged at Xavier, sent him a head nod containing the question of whether he'd be supplying this man with honey as he had Andrew.

Xavier closed his eyes and shook his head.

Maureen turned back to the man. "Oh, sorry. By the way, my name's Maureen and Andrew has told us that your name is Billy? Is that right?"

"Yeah. Yeah. Sure."

"Do you ever go by William?"

"What?"

"How about a coffee. Maybe a coffee and a donut?"

Billy snorted. "I'd just puke it up. What the fuck you want from me anyways? Are you the people who kidnapped my wife?"

"Come on, Billy. She wasn't kidnapped and you know it. And how long have you known this Vanni guy who gave you the map?"

His pale blue eyes, dotted with red and rimmed with yellow-pink lids glared at Maureen. "All right. She wasn't kidnapped. The numb c—"

"Don't you dare say that word in my presence! Call her a bitch if you will but do not use that word."

"What you gonna do about it? Bitch."

Maureen's smile and the flick of her eyebrows made him sit up straighter in his chair. He glanced over at Xavier who grinned and shrugged.

"All right. You win. The bitch took off on me. Was telling all kinds of bullshit to the cops. Lies. Lies about *me*." He stabbed a shaking index finger into his chest about where his heart would be. "ME! Lies about ME! I just want to set her straight. Get her to tell them the truth for a change. Lying bitch."

"What kind of lies about you, Billy? Can you maybe tell me some of them?"

"You know what? I want a lawyer. Right now. No more questions."

At this, a great splash at the patio made everyone, including a startled Billy, turn toward it.

Don had one arm stretched high into the air with a section at the top, a section about the size of a human hand, flapping.

"*WHAT THE FUCK?* That thing's real? It's not in m… my… muh… my imagi…"

"Oh, that's Don. Don has just volunteered to be your lawyer."

"I think we can arrange that," said Xavier as he approached Billy, hand out, to take Billy's arm. "Let me help you up. You and Don can have some time alone on the patio."

"What? What the fuck?"

"And he does this pro bono."

"The fuck. The fuck. Get your hands off me. That dude said the rum would be good luck. Because of the name of it. But I never expected to actually see one. I thought… at the elevator… I thought it was somebody in a costume… or something…"

"And what was the name of it? The rum he gave you?" Xavier asked, stifling his smile and not doing a very good job of it.

"You know?" Maureen asked Xavier.

"I have a pretty good idea. Vainy drank that all the time."

"So, Billy. What's it called?"

"Kraken. Dark rum. Brand name Kraken. And I'm not stupid. I know a kraken is kind of a giant octopus or something."

"Indeed it is. Come along, Billy. Let me introduce you." Xavier took hold of Billy's arm.

"No fucking way!"

Their change of venue to the patio was cut short by a rumble and an enormous splash about fifteen feet away from Don who was onto the patio within milli-seconds.

A huge snake-like creature leaped from the water, missing Don with its literal mouthful of oversized, icicle-like teeth but sliding away back into the dark waters with a chunk of Tovy in its mouth.

31

"NOOO!" SCREAMED MAUREEN. "Nooo!" And she ran to Tovy's side, not noticing that Billy had collapsed to the floor.

"You tend to Tovy," shouted Xavier, "and I'll get this guy over to my place. I'll be right back."

"Hurry!"

"I'll get honey," said Doctor Koi, rushing back inside.

She returned within seconds, screwed open the jar.

"The entire side of his torso is missing! There's a lung gone." Maureen leaned down. "Heart is intact but… Spleen's missing, too. A section of stomach…"

"Move. Get out of the way. Get back."

As though she were holding a set of defibrillation paddles over a cardiac patient and not a jar of honey over Tovy's damaged side, Doctor Koi called out, "Get back. Do NOT get any of this on you!"

Maureen got back.

Doctor Koi poured.

A cloud of vapor arose.

Tovy coughed, sat up and said, "Spit, damn, hell. Whoa. That was fun. NOT! Ow. Oh."

"What the hell was that thing?" asked Maureen.

"That was a moray eel. Who would have ever thought the great monster we so feared would be that species?"

"That's a moray," added Tovy, closing one eye in discomfort as he attempted to get to his feet. "What? Nobody's laughing at my joke? That's a moray. That's amore?"

"Wait, wait, wait," said Doctor Koi. "Give it a few minutes to work, Tovy. Stay there. Don't move."

"Am I seeing things? I think I'm going to faint."

"You sit down, too, Maureen. Deep breaths, OK?"

"Shit."

"Deep breaths for you, too, Tovy. You doing all right? Any pain?"

"Oh, I'd say there's pain. On a scale of one to ten, it's about a kazillion. Aiiy. Woo." His eyes widened. "Something just twitched in there. Huh. Like a balloon suddenly uh… Suddenly ballooned." He chuckled then took in a deep breath. "Ah. That's better." He tugged at what was left of his shirt. "Damn it. I liked this shirt. Oh, well. Could've been worse, I guess. I could've lost my pants. And scared hell out of you gals, eh?" He laughed. "Any ideas what brought that on? Hey, Don. You OK?"

Don crawled across the patio and with the tip of one of his arms, caressed Tovy's side. He signaled, *I'm fine. Are you?*

"Yes. I'll be good as new in no time. I'm guessing the moray detected Coco and the spiderlings from when they fell into the water. And speak of the devil. Mommy's home from shopping." He pointed toward the far end of the cavern.

And there was Coco, racing across the top of the water toward them.

"The moray eats spiders?" asked Maureen.

"Not much nutrition in these legs, eh?" Tovy laughed then grabbed his side in pain again. "It's probably because, if they're on the water, they're usually feeding on something it likes, too. Eh, Doctor Koi? Do I have that right?"

Coco was all over Tovy checking this part of him and that.

"Oh, stop it, Coco. I'm fine. I'll be fine. That tickles. Stop it."

She squatted beside him, all eyes on his face.

Tovy continued, "Coco and her species like fish. I guess when the moray sensed there were that many individuals moving around, and Don was in there making waves, too…"

Don flicked an arm, then another, then another.

"No need to apologize, Don," said Doctor Koi. "You didn't do anything wrong."

Tovy smiled in agreement. "I guess the moray figured lunch was available and up he came for a snack. I don't think their eyes are all that great."

"The species I'm familiar with tend to lash out at movement," said Doctor Koi. "Seriously though, Tovy. Are you all right? And Maureen. Quite a shocking day you've been having. You going to survive?"

Maureen got to her feet and she and Doctor Koi with one of Don's arms assisting as well—and with Coco flitting here and there all around the group—got Tovy to his feet.

From the living room came a voice, "What the hell is going on around here?"

It was Rocky.

"Just ran into Xavier with some guy who looks like he saw a ghost. And what's with all the guilty looks on your faces?" He held up his hand with something in his fingers. "Speaking of guilty, guess what I have."

☺

What Rocky had was a USB of what Officer Bob had recorded on his body cam.

"The Ottawa cops are finally starting to use those things?" asked Maureen.

"Nope."

"Is it even legal yet?"

"Who cares?" said Rocky. "We got the information we were looking for. Is Xavier coming back?"

"I am. Whatcha got there?"

"Video of our interview with Missus Muffy. Missus Harry Harrington. How about we watch this on Don's wall out on the patio? That way, we can all watch it." Rocky took a step out onto the patio where he glanced over to his left. "Oh, look. Babies. Congratulations, Coco. You must be so pleased."

Coco tapped.

"You want to watch this, too?"

Coco tapped.

Don flailed.

"What's Don saying?" asked Maureen.

"He's asking what it's going to be about. He watches a lot of TV. He and Paulo. Paulo likes cooking competitions shows. Especially…" Doctor Koi laughed. "Especially the ones when they're cooking octopus."

Paulo flicked fins.

Don flailed.

"Paulo says it's like watching a horror movie. Don likes the octopus ones, too. But, he says, not as much as Paulo does."

Don's horizontally slitted eyes turned toward Paulo and went even slittier.

"Honest to God, you guys are all nuts. Must be the honey making your brains all screwed up."

"You told her?" Rocky asked Xavier.

"She knows. Now let's see what you and Officer Bob were able to find out. Pop in the USB."

32

AS THE AREA on the patio wall above Coco and her spiderlings cleared from being merely gray rock to having blurry images of a button, a finger, a thumb, a palm, a sidewalk from Rocky's USB video on it, Don disappeared below the surface of the water beside the patio.

Staring up at Maureen, in her comfortable patio chair à la La-Z-Boy sans cushions, Paulo bobbed in the water.

"Do those things smile?" asked Maureen. "Feels like it's smiling at me."

"I believe they do," said Doctor Koi. "And I believe he is. Why? Is he making you nervous?"

"A tad. Where'd Don go?"

"If you want him to stop, that's on you. But I'd wait rather than ruin a developing friendship."

"You're absolutely certain Tovy will be OK on his own?"

Doctor Koi covered her smile. "Xavier's right. You do like to change the subject."

No response other than a raised eyebrow.

"Tovy will be fine," said Doctor Koi. "Absolutely fine. He merely needs rest right now. The pain will dissipate shortly. It would be similar to a burn patient's experience as the nerves are regenerated. I'm sure you're familiar with that?"

"I am," said Maureen.

"Although it feels like it takes forever, it's over relatively quickly because of the honey's properties. And by 'rest,' I mean, a nap. He's already back to normal. All his systems are go. He'll relax for a while until his innards have renewed their supply of bacteria. Bacteria do their own thing, though. The honey doesn't affect them in any way."

A flash of clusterwinks spread along the shore. Here and there, Don's arms popped out of the water as he scooped the tiny creatures from their bed.

"Do you want me to put this on pause, Don?" Xavier called out.

Under the water Don went again to pop up beside Paulo. Right arm, *Yes.*

"He does this every single time we get together for a movie," said Rocky. "I love the guy."

"Does what?"

Xavier leaned down from his patio chair to tap an invisible button on the patio floor beside him. The video paused on the image of a door knocker with a large, strong-fingered hand reaching for it. "Go ahead, Don."

In no time, Don was beside Maureen dumping clusterwinks into her lap.

"Ew. God."

Don formed a laugh emoji.

Xavier, Doctor Koi and Rocky laughed. In the water, Paulo slapped.

"What does he expect me to do with these things?"

Don flailed, formed a laugh emoji, carefully collected the cluster-winks from Maureen's lap and slid away into the water again. There, he placed a clusterwink into Paulo's mouth, then an arm went underwater to put one into his own.

"Oh for fuck's sake!"

"Yup," laughed Xavier. "Octopus popcorn."

"Oh my God. I'm sure I must be actually dead and I'm in hell."

Laughter on the patio, happy slaps on the water.

The video resumed.

It took two sets of knocks before the huge wooden door swung open to reveal an attractive blonde in her late fifties or early sixties.

A flash of the rear side of a badge.

The woman's eyes glanced at the front of it and widened.

"Missus Harrington?" asked a deep voice, most likely that of Officer Bob. "Missus Harry Harrington?"

"I am."

"Let's do this all casual-like. Let's call me Bob and this guy here…" The camera swung to Rocky at chest level. "… is Rocky."

"Who invented the body cam anyway?" Maureen asked nobody in particular. "Those things are awesome."

Splashing.

Doctor Koi's voice, "A body cam is a small video camera that some cops wear in the United States."

Splashing.

"I don't think they wear them up here yet. Legally at least."

Splashing.

"Probably is. I think they need permission, or at least a warrant, to audio record but I think it's legal for the—"

Splashing.

"Don," said Rocky.

The video stopped.

A single splash.

"Shut up. Watch the video."

The sound of a bubble bursting as it popped up from under the water.

"Don?" This was Xavier.

A flick of water onto the patio missed Xavier by inches.

Xavier leaned down to tap the patio floor. The video resumed.

The woman beckoned Officer Bob and Rocky into a huge dining room to the right of the entrance door. There was a flash of kitchen through the doorway at the far wall. She indicated they sit. The table between them screamed expensive.

"What can I do for you, officers? Campaigning the neighborhood for funds or something? My husband usually gives at the office." Her eyes blinked as she stared at a spot slightly above camera level. Where Officer Bob's eyes would be.

"Can you tell me where you were yesterday?"

"Uh. Do I need a lawyer or something?" Her mouth semi-smiled, then closed as she pushed her chin slightly forward.

"No, no, of course not, Missus Harrington. Relax. We need to ask you some questions. That's all. Then we'll be on our way." The view shifted. "Isn't that right, Rocky?"

"Yes, sir. It is. Absolutely."

"So where were you yesterday?"

"Yesterday? I was on my friend's yacht."

"And which yacht would that be?"

It wasn't quite a laugh came from the woman, it was more of a gasp-laugh. "I think it's called Fannie's Farce or something like that. Why are you ask—?"

"So this male 'friend' will verify your alibi?"

"Male? No! Good heavens, no. I'm married. I was with friends. Girl friends. Female friends. And... and ... and ... Alibi? What alibi? What do I need an alibi for?"

"I'm the one asking the questions, ma'am. How many of your so-called friends were on this... this yacht?"

"There were five of us and it is a yacht and what's it to you, anyway? I don't understand why you're asking all these questions. We went on a tour. That's all."

"A tour. To where?"

"To nowhere. Just along the Rideau Canal. We do it often. It's a... It's a girls' night out."

"So it wasn't just a coincidence then that you perhaps had some evidence to toss overboard?"

"What?"

"She's good, isn't she?" said On-Camera-Rocky.

"Darn tootin', she is."

"What are you officers going on about? Why are you here? What are all these questions?"

"Well," said Officer Bob. "We have some bad news for you. Or maybe it's not such bad news in your case."

"Go easy, Bob."

"Bad news?" Her eyes blinked faster.

"About Harry. Your husband."

"Oh?" Redness crept up from her jaw and her eyes twitched. "Bad... news...?"

Maureen giggled. "Botoxed forehead. She can't frown."

"I'm sorry, ma'am, but he was found deceased on Rideau Street."

The woman's hand leaped to her cleavage. "No."

"Yes," said Officer Bob. "Dead as a fucking doornail."

"Jeez," said On-Camera-Rocky's voice, and as he leaned toward Officer Bob's body cam, his face came into full view. "Take it easy with the—"

Splashing.

Don was on the patio within nanoseconds to slap the spot on the patio floor that stopped the video. He was at the wall and tapping the image of Rocky's face then back to the physical Rocky, pointing to him and pointing at the image then at Paulo who was slapping and splashing the water.

"No, I'm not a famous movie star now, Don. This is a video. Not a movie. People on the Surface do this all the time with their cell phones. Go on. Get back in the water. Stop interrupting."

Don caressed Rocky's face, tapped the floor, then slid into the water where Paulo slid a flipper over him. Don slid the tip of his arm over Paulo's head.

Xavier tapped the patio floor.

"Yes, ma'am. Murdered. Brutally murdered."

"Um, Bob?" came On-Camera-Rocky's voice again. "I wouldn't use the word brutally. He wasn't beaten or anything. Uh, ma'am? We think he was poisoned. Poisoned with zombie powder."

"Oh, come on." The woman's face lit up with a semi-questioning smile. "That's only in the movies. Is this some kind of Candid Camera thing or something?" She swayed from side to side looking past Officer Bob's body-cam perspective. She adjusted the front of her blouse.

"No ma'am. It's true. Somebody is poisoning men with zombie powder and we have evidence that it's you."

"*Me?* What men? I only—"

"Aha."

On-Camera-Rocky said, "Gotcha."

"This means life imprisonment, no parole for probably sixty years, ma'am. Maybe even the death penalty."

"The dea— They don't do the death penalty in Canada! What are you talk—"

"The pills, ma'am. Who did you get the pills from?"

The woman crossed her arms and leaned against her chair's back. "I didn't get anything from anybody."

On-Camera-Rocky said, "As we suspected. She made them herself. And then she distributed them to her friends so they could kill their husbands, too."

"I do believe you're right, Rocky. Does she look guilty to you?"

"She sure does, Bob. Are we going to take her downtown to question her? Where all the reporters hang out?"

The woman gasped then patted her hair with both hands. "Please. Let me get freshened up first. And I didn't do anything. Anything at all." She stood up from her chair. "I'll just be a minute."

"SIT!" demanded Officer Bob. "You're not going to be slipping out of our sight to get rid of the evidence. No way."

"No way," added On-Camera-Rocky.

"I was just going to get my lawyer's business card. I don't have any evidence to get rid of. That's silly. I don't." She pointed in the direction of the kitchen doorway. "Can I please just—"

"No."

"You don't want to piss this guy off," said On-Camera-Rocky. "You might as well just tell us. Start at the beginning. It's easiest that way. Right, Bob?"

"Right, Rocky. Go ahead, honey. Spill."

The woman sat back down. "Her name is Va-Va-Vamoose. Like… Her Facebook name, I mean. I met her. I mean online I met her. Maybe a month ago."

A movement of Officer Bob's body cam showed him handing his cell phone to On-Camera-Rocky. Then a quiet "Check her out."

The body cam swung back to Missus Harrington. "She runs a… Like a… Like a sort of AA group but it's not AA, it's like the other one, the Al Anon one? But it's not for alcoholics. I mean people who live with alcoholics. It's… It's…" The woman fanned her face with both hands as her eyes strained ceiling-ward.

"Relax, ma'am. Take a breath."

The woman closed her eyes. She inhaled deeply. She placed her palms together at chest level. Held her breath for one, two, three seconds and slowly exhaled out of her closed-lips' mouth.

"Did that work, ma'am?"

"Yes. Sorry."

"No need to be sorry, ma'am. Carry on. Just the facts, ma'am. Just the facts."

Maureen giggled. "Seriously? Dragnet?"

"He's good, isn't he?" said Doctor Koi, giggling, too.

"It's kind of a group for women whose husbands cheat on them. We all go by fake names on there. Va-Va picks them for us. I'm Pinky Pearl. Va-Va works at that Italian church on Rochester sometimes and she has weekly evening meetings at the Adult High School. But she says we can't go to any of those."

"Oh really. Why is that, ma'am?"

"Oh, in case we get spotted or recognized by each other or whatever. I forget what she actually said word for word."

"You realize, of course, that there's no such group either at the Italian church or at the Adult High School. That's very naughty of you to suggest anything untoward about either of those places."

"What's that? But she said… She said she worked there."

The scene on the wall expanded as Officer Bob obviously had placed his elbows on the table and leaned forward. "Just because people say they do things doesn't mean they actually do. Or just because people say they didn't do things doesn't mean they actually didn't. Have you never met a liar before?"

"Liar? Uh." The woman's eyes went left then right then flicked very briefly to where Officer Bob's eyes would be then away just as quickly. "Of course, I have. I'm not stupid."

The scene shifted back to its original size. "You didn't find it odd that she was wanting to insure you gals never got together? To perhaps discuss what was really going on? To question?"

"She said we should keep everything secret. Even from each other."

"And you're certain this is a woman."

"Yes. She understands what it's like to be cheated on. She said so. She posted that she developed this product that when somebody takes it— Oh, dear. It probably isn't legal, is it?"

"Don't worry about that right now. Just keep talking."

"Oh. Oh, dear. I thought she was actually for real but…"

"But?"

"Well she told us this stuff would make our husband love only us if he took it. She says it worked for her husband and she hasn't been happier. It's some kind of chemical that makes some kind of brain chemical do something and it would make him faithful forever."

Officer Bob's laugh made the woman jump.

"What?" she asked.

"Kind of a revisit to the marriage vow?"

"Marriage vow?"

"Till death do us part."

"Oh. Oh no. Oh." The woman's hand clasped the front of her blouse.

On-Camera-Rocky's voice: "Jesus, Bob."

"So where did you get your hands on these pills?"

"A man. She sent a man to give them to me."

"Description please."

"Kinda short. It was dark. Two o'clock in the morning. By that Italian church." She ran a knuckle along the underside of one eye. "Are you sure there's no group like that at that church? Or nobody like that? Helping out women whose husbands…? You know." Her lower lip quivered.

"Absolutely certain."

"So I was wrong to believe her then?"

"Wronger than wrong. For somebody not so innocent, you're awfully innocent, aren't you?"

"Are you making fun of me?"

"No. I am not. Keep going on the description of this man."

The knuckle wiped something away from the bottom lid of her other eye. She sighed. "I was supposed to meet him by those steps that lead up—or down, depending, I guess—to the parking lot. Behind the church?"

"Yes. I know the spot."

"Is there anything you *don't* know?"

"In this neighborhood? No."

"That's true," said On-Camera-Rocky. "Hundred percent true."

The woman's eyes moved to where On-Camera-Rocky's eyes would be. "But I wasn't to go into the parking lot where—when I think of it now—where it would have been brighter. I could sort of see his face anyway though and he looked kind of familiar. Is that maybe why she didn't want me to see him? Maybe I might recognize him?"

"What do you think?"

The woman shrugged. "But he didn't look the same as I remember him. He was in good shape and clean-shaven. He wasn't like that before. He's even kind of nice looking. But in a creepy way if that makes any sense"

"It does."

"He looked… Uh. Am I a racist if I say he looked Italian?"

"Not if he does."

"And he… The really creepy thing about him was that he seemed to have no… What do you call it? No personal distance zone. And it was like he was reading me or something. Like, he was smiling but his eyes were… Ugh." She shivered.

"Could he possibly have been masquerading as a woman on Face-book? As this Va-Va-Voom?"

"Va-Va-Vamoose is her name. Oh dear. Oh dear. I made a big mistake, didn't I?"

"You did."

The body cam turned to On-Camera-Rocky again, holding Officer Bob's cell phone, its screen showing the standard shadow person of a Facebook member with no photo. The top line of text below the shadow person showed the top half of the name, Vanni Smith.

A large hand snatched the phone away from On-Camera-Rocky's hand and all hands plus the phone disappeared. The body cam turned back to the woman

"Got him. We'll find out where he is later. Right?" The chuckle from Officer Bob was echoed by On-Camera-Rocky.

"I wonder where that could be," said On-Camera-Rocky.

Laughter.

The scene jumped around as Officer Bob rose from his chair.

"Thank you for all this information, Missus Harrington. Much appreciated. Appreciated far more than you'll ever know."

The body cam view turned toward the hallway then toward the front door.

"And by the way, he isn't dead, but he's out of your life forever. You can rest assured of that."

"What?"

"You tell ANYONE and I mean *ANYONE* about our little talk today, and I *will* be reporting you to the police for attempted murder. Which is what you actually did. Didn't you?"

The body cam turned back to the ghost-white face of Missus Harrington, attempted murderer.

"Because we know exactly where Muffy is and you don't."

The body cam video went blank.

33

WAVING OF QUEEN'S antennas, clicking of Coco's feet, flailing of Don's arms and Doctor Koi translating. "'I don't know how your timeframes work, but I would say before you brought those men below but not since.'"

"That does it then," said Xavier. "It has to be Pamela's husband."

"I wouldn't be so sure of that," said Tovy, rubbing his side, the one that had been damaged by the giant moray eel. "I think he would have outright killed her. That's what he tried the last time. And that cave up there—wherever it is—doesn't show up on the map he gave Billy."

"True enough. But do you think Vainy would be stupid enough to drill into the bottom of that cave when he knows— At least he *must* have a good idea there are creatures living below if he was able to produce a map that brought those men down here, right? It means he's been here."

"I doubt if he knows about the wildlife down here," offered Rocky. "You know how they can be totally invisible unless you're actually looking for them. Even if you know they're here. And I can't imagine he has any idea about the uranium."

"I agree," said Tovy.

"I think maybe you're right," said Xavier. "No matter who's drilling up there, they can't possibly know about the uranium. Instant death. If it's Vainy and he's trying to take over our lucrative living conditions down here, he wouldn't risk it. It would defeat the purpose. One thing he isn't, is stupid."

"'And speaking of the one called Vainy,'" signed Queen, "'… do you have any idea where he is right now?'"

"We don't."

"'Will that human female survive her injuries?'"

"She will, Queen. She's been taking your honey for a long time."

"'What would you do without me?'" Queen's tiny black eyes drifted to Maureen.

Xavier moved to shield Maureen from Queen's gaze. He bowed. "Once we find that human female, she'll survive. But we have to find her soon. With the greatest respect, Queen, we appreciate all you've done for us in the past, but if you could find it in your heart to tell us where she is, we would appreciate it. May the future continue with peace between us."

A flick of antenna and Queen and her entourage exited across the ceiling and out and up the patio's overhang.

☺

"We have to find Vainy and fast. We can't have Queen and her warriors find him first. Get everybody Topside out searching. But don't tell them why."

"What's the problem, Xavier?" asked Maureen. "Wouldn't that be a good thing if she helps us out?"

"No, it wouldn't, dear girl. If she finds him, we'll owe her yet another favor."

34

"**LOOK WHO'S HERE,**" squealed Sandra as she rushed from the Topside kitchen toward Maureen and Doctor Koi, both wearing small backpacks. She threw her arms around Maureen with her gloved hands held up and out, and hugged with her elbows. She elbow-hugged Doctor Koi for nearly five beats.

"It's so good to see you guys. Sit. Sit. But over here at the counter so we can talk." She indicated the stools at the counter that separated the eating area from the kitchen.

Adjusting her beanie-like sous chef hat, she scampered around behind the counter where she reached down to bring out—one in each hand, like a magician—two placemats with smiley faces on them.

"What can I get yaz?" She smiled at each of them. "Let me see… Maureen. I think coffee. Yes?"

"Sounds good to me."

"And Doctor Koi? Tea?"

"What self-respecting old Chinese woman doesn't drink tea? This one. I'll have hot chocolate, if you don't mind."

"Ah. Of course. Sorry. My bad. It wasn't because of your race, it was because of your age that I... uh... Sorry."

Doctor Koi covered her laugh. "Don't be. You should hear what goes on in my head sometimes about you young folks. Or maybe you shouldn't. Do you have any?"

"That sounds good," said Maureen. "I'll have the hot choc—"

"You will not!" called Missus Cheffie, waving a metal lifter in the air at the rear of the kitchen. "If you want anything sweet... I mean, anything *sweet* like that, get the hell up to the Surface for it. It's much safer."

"I wouldn't have let her have it," said Sandra, almost pouting. "I know what's in it."

"Of course you do, dear. But we have to be careful."

A chair scraped in the seating area, then another, indicating that two more customers had arrived.

"Be right with yaz," called Sandra.

"Take your time, Sandy."

"Why do people call me that?" Sandra grumbled. "My dad called me that when he got in his cups." She reached under the counter and produced two mugs. One of them she took to the tall coffee machine where she filled it. "Have you decided to become civilized yet? Or do you still want sugar in this?"

"I still want sugar. Please."

Sandra brought the mug back and placed it in front of Maureen. One hand went under the counter and up came a handful of sugar packets. "Not only will that stuff rot your teeth, but it will shorten your life. You, of all people should know *that*, Nurse Maureen."

"I do, but I like to live dangerously at least once a day. Beats dying of boredom. And I see this is cane sugar. Healthy as hell, so what's your problem?" Faking a sneer at Sandra, she flipped the little packet back and forth in her finger and thumb before tearing it open and dumping it into her coffee. "Two should do it." She picked up another packet while keeping her gaze steady on Sandra.

Leaning to the side and calling out to those in the seating area, Sandra thumb-pointed at Maureen. "I've been trying to save this lady's life for nearly seventy years and look at the gratitude I get."

The twelve scattered customers applauded.

"And now, Madame Doctor Koi. A mug of hot chocolate for you." Sandra snatched up the other mug from the countertop, opened the cupboard under the coffee machine and brought out a huge, lidded jar which she unscrewed. "Two percent or homo?"

"Homo. Always." Doctor Koi did not cover her smile.

"Do you not have a menu?" asked Maureen. "Or am I missing something?" She turned to look at the other tables. No one held a menu. No table displayed one.

"We tend to have Missus Cheffie make what she wants and then we get to choose," said Doctor Koi, taking her mug of hot chocolate from Sandra. "Thanks."

"So what are the choices today?"

"Blueberry pancakes."

"And?"

"Blueberry pancakes."

"I thought you said we would have a choice."

"You do," said Missus Cheffie, flipping one over on the big black stovetop. "The choice is, take it, or leave it."

"I should have seen that one coming," said Maureen, trying to hide an embarrassed grin. "Blueberry pancakes it is. And for your information, I would have chosen blueberry pancakes no matter what else might have been available."

"That's exactly what all my customers say when I make them. So what's the point of preparing anything else?" Missus Cheffie's laugh triggered another round of applause from the seating area.

From Doctor Koi's small purse came a now-familiar jingle. She answered. "Any luck?"

A lengthy pause.

"Awesome." She tapped her phone off and slipped it into her purse. "Rocky found Pamela."

Cheers erupted from the seating area.

"He's with her now. But he needs us to help get her out. He doesn't want to jiggle anything. In case he causes more damage." She slipped off the counter stool. "You, too, Sandra. We need somebody strong."

"Go, go," said Missus Cheffie.

"Want me to help?" came a male voice from among the seated customers.

"That would be wonderful, Jean-Pierre," said Missus Cheffie. "Thank you. Come get your pancakes. Maple syrup is already on your table, I see. You need a fork though."

"I meant—"

"Yeah, yeah. And on your way, bring the dirty dishes from that table beside you."

"I…"

In the background, at the far wall, Maureen, Sandra and Doctor Koi were in the process of disappearing down the corridor there. Barely overheard was Doctor Koi's voice, "Hope you brought your Gravol, gals. It's going to be a bumpy ride."

35

"**THIS ISN'T THE** same way we came in," said Maureen.

"It isn't. This one is more like a direct flight."

"That's funny," said Sandra.

Doctor Koi made no response.

"Isn't it? Funny I mean?"

"When the termants first learned about the construction going on in your neighborhood, they were very concerned." She touched the wall and a panel slid open to reveal the regular tube-shaped elevator that Maureen and Sandra were becoming used to but it was set sideways and with four seats at one end and a clear space at the other. "You don't need to strap in but be prepared for some G-force going on."

"G force?"

"Ever go on a ride called the Tilt-A-Whirl?"

"Ah. Yes. I remember," said Maureen. "That's the one where the seats go around while the thing goes around."

"I meant the one you stood up in."

"Yup. Been on that one, too. Why do you ask?"

"The pressure… Take a seat. The pressure will be similar. We are going to be traveling fast. Do you know where we are? Any idea?"

"Underground," laughed Sandra.

Doctor Koi touched the wall.

The panel slid closed. The elevator itself became dark but the light glowing around its seams provided enough illumination for the passengers to see any instrument panels, and each other.

"Ready?"

"Let 'er rip," said Sandra.

"Do we have a choice?"

Doctor Koi sat in another of the chairs and touched the wall.

The elevator made no sound but the three women were pushed into their chair backs.

"What are we underground under then?" asked Maureen.

"We were under the Rideau Centre. More or less. But now I'd say we are probably just going below Somerset and Bronson. And we are rising as we go…"

"Cool," said Sandra.

"And here we are."

The panel slid open to reveal a dark, cement-block basement. An overhead light flickered on. The women exited.

"The stairs are over here."

"Oh," said Maureen. "I know where we are. That's Gladstone up there."

Behind her, the cement-like door that Doctor Koi had just closed, showed no indication whatsoever that there was a door even there, it was camouflaged so perfectly into what appeared to be merely the edge section of the building it was attached to.

Into her phone, Doctor Koi said, "We're here. We'll be there in two shakes."

On foot, they rounded the corner onto Gladstone. Up ahead, an ancient, white, Dodge cargo van had been backed up onto the vacant lot on this side of the construction site that Maureen and Sandra had only yesterday slid into.

On the side of the van, a magnetic sign read:

CLAN-
DESTINEY
CONSTRUCTION

Behind the van, a small, walled construction tent sat, obscuring anything from three points of view. The van was close enough to the street side of the tent to prevent any passing traffic, either vehicular, cycle or foot, to see inside by way of the fourth point of view.

A man, a man with long hair and scruffy clothes, stood there, waving at them.

"Who's that?" asked Maureen.

"That's Rocky as Jerome. This is his spot to keep an eye on things. As you are fully aware, ladies, the construction the City is doing here is dangerously close to the world of the termants. He has to play homeless druggie to get away with it. He reports in on a regular basis."

"Oh. Right. The guy we heard when we were in that pit, Maureen."

"That's him? That's Rocky? Good disguise. I'd never recognize him."

"Hey," he said. "She was in rough shape but I managed to get some honey into her so she's coming around. But we have to get her down to Topside sooner than soon."

"Any sign of Vainy," asked Doctor Koi.

"Not yet. But it is him. For sure. He's the driller. The drill's even down there. He's got some kind of generator down there, too. He's the one who pushed Pamela down into the cave. He must have given her a goddamn good shove. Look."

Doctor Koi swung her backpack around, extracted a flashlight, and they looked.

The cave was the size of a Chateau Laurier ballroom but its "floor" lay at a thirty-degree angle. Easy enough to maneuver up and down. But not if a person tripped on the way. Or was pushed.

The group made their way below to where Pamela lay, eyes blinking, mouth managing a smile. "You're here. Thanks."

Beside her was a coffin-like plywood box with low sides. A few plumbing pipes lay inside.

Rocky pointed at the box. "I didn't want to try to get her into that. Her arm seems to be broken. She says she can't move so I was afraid of hurting her neck or something."

"The honey didn't work?" asked Maureen.

"Too close to the Surface."

"Oh."

"Didn't Xavier explain all that to you?"

Maureen ignored him. "We can all do this together," she said. "But first, let's make a neck brace for her. Anybody got anything that will work? And why not a stretcher? That thing must be heavy as hell. And what's with the pipes?"

"We set this up like this to make it look like repairs are going on to gas lines. A stretcher would make people look. A box with pipes sticking out of it would make them *not* pay attention. Right?"

"True enough," said Maureen. "Where'd you get the van?"

"No, Maureen," smiled Rocky. "It isn't stolen. Officer Bob has a lot of connections. There's a guy named Rick who procures any vehicles we need. On loan. Construction stuff, too. Some on loan, some not, but all on the up and up. Don't worry."

"He did the sign for the van, too?" She bent down beside Pamela. "Ready?"

"Ready," chorused the others.

"One, two, *three*."

Pamela was up and into the coffin-like stretcher. Pipes were placed to make it appear to be a toolbox, and up the slope they went, two to a side, to the back of the van where they slid her in.

"Not the sign, no. Pamela here is an amazing artist and we have somebody who's a magician when it comes to cutting out that magnetic stuff. Rick gets it for us. Through Officer Bob, though. Everything we get from the Surface is through Officer Bob. We have every sign you can imagine stored away Topside."

Once in the van, Maureen checked the makeshift neck brace that curled around below Pamela's chin, Sandra's yellow rain gear that had been in the backpack Maureen had been given. "Feels OK to you?"

"I'm good. Thanks. You're an angel."

Sandra, patting Maureen on the shoulder, said, "You wouldn't say that if you knew her better."

"Oh, stop." Maureen laughed. "So we're off to the hospital then?"

"Topside hospital. She won't last much longer at Surface level, remember?"

"Oh. Right. So we're going to drive to… the Rideau Centre?"

"No. Back to where we came up from. Where the elevator is. Do you have a license?"

"I do," said Sandra. "I'll drive. It's not even a block but we can't take any chances, can we?"

From the back of the van, Rocky pulled out another section of construction tent and propped it against the others. He snapped two clips on each end of it. "Can you guys handle getting her out of the van and down to the elevator? I should really stick around here in case you-know-who shows up, eh? And make sure I've gotten rid of any telltale signs that anybody was here. Except for the absence of Pamela that is. I hope he'll just assume she crawled out on her own."

"I think so," Doctor Koi said. "It's down hill all the way." She dug into her purse and removed the small plastic taser she'd put in there the day before.

"Ah. Good idea. Thanks." Rocky tucked it away into his back pocket. "If you can't manage—but I'm sure you can—just text. Better to text so I won't have to talk in case somebody shows up. I won't want them to recognize my voice, will I?"

"You'll contact Xavier if or when he shows up?"

"That I will. Just leave the keys in the van. Don't lock it. Stay safe."

"Stay safe."

"And Pamela?"

"Uh huh?"

"Get well. And fast. Promise?"

"Promise."

Rocky shut the back door of the van and banged on it twice.

36

IN NO TIME, they were in the Two Guys' Room, which would now, for certain, be called The Hospital by all and sundry. Even though it was only one room.

"Um. Where did Muffy go? He didn't... Uh."

"He's fine, Maureen," said Stan as he and Barry and the three women got Pamela out of the toolbox onto a bed. "As fine as he can be, that is. He's safely locked away in one of the recovery rooms. We're fillin' up fast!"

"Is that a hint?" asked the man sitting on the side of the other bed, taking everything in, staring at Maureen and Sandra. It was Theo.

"Recovery rooms?" asked Doctor Koi.

"Down below where they've always been."

"Ah. Of course, Xavier's famous recovery rooms."

"All three are now at full capacity."

"Those women are new?" asked Theo. "Or do I have dementia?"

Stan began hooking Pamela up to the machines near her bed so Stan pointed the top of his head at them as he said their names. "They're new, yes. No dementia, but we want to keep an eye on you for a while longer. There are tests we'd like to run and run again. Maureen helped us out when you were found."

"He's looking really good," said Maureen. "Looks like there were no aftereffects from the… the, uh… the substance he was given."

"It's OK, I know what he gave me. I know what it's called. It was zombie powder. And I'm feeling totally one hundred percent now. Except for one thing." The corner of his mouth twitched. "So, Sandra is it? You're the one helping Missus Cheffie out in the kitchen now?"

"That I am. Is there something I can get you?"

"If you wouldn't mind. I've had the strongest urge for something ever since he gave me that stuff. It's an almost unbearable urge."

"Sure. Name it."

"Could you guys maybe rustle me up a plate of brains?"

Theo, Stan and even Barry burst into laughter.

"He'll be good company for Pamela, I think," said Doctor Koi from behind her fingers.

"We got him," said Xavier from the doorway. "Rocky got him. Tased him. Good plan to give your gun to him, Doctor Koi."

Xavier gave her a thumb's up, but she stepped forward for a high five. Which, of course, for long, lanky Xavier was a medium-high five but they both threw arms around each other and hugged.

"We gotta get there right away, though. Rocky thinks all that screeching Vainy did probably drew attention. Both up here and down where our friends the termants reside."

37

ON THEIR WAY back to Seaside the long way, with Vainy in plasticuffs—"Let me guess, you got those from Officer Bob, too? Is there anything that man won't provide for you?"

"Not much," said Rocky.

"Nothing so far," said Xavier. "Stop wiggling around, Vainy. You wanna get tased again?"

"Fuck you."

"No thanks."

A lurch.

The elevator had come to a stop.

The panel slid open without a sound.

Under the dim overhead lights of the cave stood about two dozen warrior termants. One of them, the one in front, was Bear-Trap.

Bear-Trap flicked its antennas.

Vainy's gasp of surprise and fear was overridden by Maureen's so went unnoticed by anyone.

Bear-Trap stepped forward toward Maureen and reached out one of its front legs toward her, to touch her, but she stepped back in time. Xavier pushed her back even further and said, "Hands off. Or, feet off, I guess that would be. What are you doing? Why have you stopped us?"

Bear-Trap's antennas and legs flicked and tapped.

"What's it saying?" asked Maureen.

"Don't ask me," said Rocky. "Far's I know, Coco's the only one who can interpret what these things are saying. Xavier? Any idea?"

"Not a one."

"I know."

All eyes turned toward Vainy.

"That thing is saying it wants this woman to go with them. And you're to release me. She's the one you want. Er, the one they want. The one who was drilling in the hole there. I just found it. And I got accused." His glare did not make Rocky turn away as expected, because Vainy's empty stare quickly shot to the floor.

"I doubt that very much," said Xavier.

Flickering antennas and taps came from not only Bear-Trap, but from several of its companions as well.

"Do you know this man?" Maureen asked Bear-Trap.

A tap of left front foot.

"Is that a no?"

A tap of right front foot.

"So you can tell us yes and no like Don does?"

A tap of right front foot.

"Cool!" She grabbed Xavier's arm. "We can communicate with them."

"Is this man a friend of yours?" Xavier asked Bear-Trap.

A tap of left front foot.

"That's a no?"

A tap of right front foot.

"That does it then," said Xavier. "How about we conclude this meeting and convene again in Doctor Koi's apartment?"

Bear-Trap turned to his companions then back toward the group in the elevator.

A tap of right front foot from each of them.

The panel slid closed and after a slight—almost imperceptibly slight—pressure, the elevator was on the move again.

38

"**SO YOU ARE** definitely, absolutely, one hundred percent sure he's the one?" asked Doctor Koi.

Vainy, still in plasticuffs and seated on the floor of Doctor Koi's apartment, said, "I have no idea on earth what you people are talking about. Just know, that whatever it is, I had nothing to do with it. Not a single thing. It was this woman..." He indicated Maureen with his right shoulder. "... and her lesbo buddy here..." He indicated Sandra with his left shoulder. "... who are, as you call it, definitely, absolutely, one hundred percent behind all of it. Trust me. I know. I know everything that's been going on here. I get the transmissions, too."

"So you know all about Muffy, then?" asked Xavier.

"Mu—? Who? Huh? Uh. Oh. Wait. Yes. Of course, I do. She killed him with a medical enhancement." Again, Vainy's right shoulder hitched toward Maureen. "One she had illegal possession of. It didn't go with his heart medication and the wine he took. She killed him. Careless fool.

I knew all that. Same as you, Xavier. Same as you, too, Rocky. Doctor Koi."

At this, Coco scampered over to where Vainy was sitting. Slowly, she turned her head one way then another while her double row of eyes examined the area where his buttocks touched the floor.

Splashing from the patio area that Doctor Koi translated, while laughing, as, "Don't say it, Coco. Please don't say it."

"Say what?" asked Maureen.

Coco tapped.

Don flailed.

Doctor Koi opened her mouth to translate but Maureen was already laughing. "Oh my God. You guys are hilarious."

"What are you talking about?" demanded Vainy.

Tapping, flailing, and Doctor Koi translating: "Coco says it must be a myth that liars' pants catch on fire because your pants are fine."

"Yikes!" said Vainy. "What the f—"

Queen dropped to the floor with her entourage. "This is he?" she signed.

Bear-Trap, sans companions, sidled up to her.

"It is," said Doctor Koi.

"But we would prefer the female behind Xavier."

"Why is that?" asked Doctor Koi.

"She has had no honey. That means we can administer our special honey to her and…"

"Go on," said Xavier. "Please, with all due respect." He bowed his head. "The male human needs to know what your special honey does."

"He *needs* to?"

Xavier smiled. "Let's just say I want him to know."

Queen's left rear foot kicked out and shook several times.

"That one I do know," said Xavier. "She's laughing."

"Why?" asked Maureen. "And what does the special honey do?"

"The special honey would extend your life while…"

"While?"

"Uh." Xavier's eyes went to Queen.

She tapped once with her right front foot.

"The special honey would extend your life while the nymphs feasted on your body. You would regener—"

"WHAT?"

"You would constantly regenerate. But without pain. In fact, you'd be in a kind of trance state the entire time. And you'd be… What's the word? Releasable?"

"Well, that's nice of her."

Xavier's voice dropped to a whisper. "Keep it respectful. Or we'll all be in trouble. Releasable but… Somewhat like a fine wine."

"Xavier? Quit stalling. What are you saying?"

"Like a fine wine. Aged. Alive but… suffering from the consequences."

"So. There. See?" said Vainy. "She doesn't want me. I'm no good to her."

"Uh, actually, Vainy, it goes deeper than that," Xavier said. "She's a very kind, caring… uh… sovereign. She is wanting to save *you* unnecessary pain. See… The nymphs need to feed on those who have received the special honey. Regardless. If you add special honey to the regular honey, there would be *no* absence of pain. With regular honey, as you have probably experienced a few times, Vainy—that time you cut your finger, for instance—healing is pretty much instant, but the pain is… not so nice. And not so instant. And since nobody is allowed painkillers because of their addiction issues, there are none available anywhere in this world. I'm sure you can imagine what you would be dealing with."

"But you're not going to do that, though," said Vainy, a thin bead of perspiration at the top of his forehead. "You wouldn't. You're a doctor. 'Do no harm.'"

"But I wouldn't be doing any harm, would I? I would be doing something good. Something wonderful. I would be saving this entire world down here by helping the nymphs survive to continue with the future survival of their species."

Xavier turned toward Queen. "I think Vainy would be an—"

"Don't call me that!"

"I think Vainy would be an excellent choice for the warrior section."

Bear-Trap tapped all its feet and flicked its antennas.

Queen signed, "'I agree and so does the leader of the warriors. Take him.'"

Amid Vainy's screams of protest and tears of apology, several workers gathered around him and carried him off along the wall to the ceiling then out and up the overhang and away.

Bear-Trap approached Xavier to stand on its back two legs. It stretched its front right leg to reach the offered palm of Xavier.

"I guess this is a high three?" Xavier laughed.

Bear-Trap dropped to the floor and shook its right hind foot vigorously. It turned but before it left, it scuttled to Maureen where it once again rose to its hind legs. With its front leg, it caressed her cheek.

Bear-Trap dropped down, shot up the wall along the ceiling and out and up the overhang.

Queen's eyes had been on Maureen the entire time.

"With all due respect, Queen," said Xavier, again stepping in front of Maureen. "We do have another specimen for you."

All antennas stood erect and rigid.

Xavier turned. "Bring him in, Stan."

Stan appeared at the doorway with a very groggy, shaking Billy. "Here he is."

"He's had no honey," said Xavier to Queen. "None whatsoever. He is the one responsible for the human female being down here living in constant fear. Fear of him. He has beaten her so badly, we weren't sure if even your honey would regenerate the damages done to her body let alone to her face. We ask of you, with all due respect…" Xavier bowed his head.

Queen tapped her right front leg.

"Please take him and feed him both honeys. Allow him to live forever while being fed on by—not neutrals, but by female young only."

Tapping and flicking of antennas.

Doctor Koi translated, "She said, 'Consider it done.'"

39

"OH, HELL YES," said Missus Cheffie. "Here on Topside, we all know what goes on down there. We've all been down there at some point or another, right?"

The entire cafeteria area was crowded with patrons so the applause was loud and echoed everywhere. Tovy and Rocky smiled from the stools at the counter.

"Most of us don't know exactly how far down we were when we were there, but we know. Some of us have even seen the bugs down there."

"Big buggers of bugs," called out Jean-Pierre. "C'est vrai?"

"Vrai, is right," muttered a couple of his buddies who were standing beside him. "Truer than true, in fact."

"And that, I think, was one of Xavier's most brilliant moves to help us get off whatever drug or bad habit we were on," continued Missus Cheffie.

Murmurs of approval.

"Of course, the honey helped, but I'm sure you know what I mean. But listen, sweetie, Sandra here has already promised not to let Xavier know we know." With her arm behind Sandra, Missus Cheffie squeezed her shoulder. "Right?"

"Right," said Sandra, adjusting her beanie-like sous chef hat.

"Aren't you coming to the Surface with me?" asked Maureen.

"I'll see you later at your place. I've got me a part-time job here. And there, too." She pointed to the Topside Hospital entranceway where Stan and Barry stood alongside Pamela who was on a gurney with Theo sitting beside her. "I've already been home and back a few times."

On the other side of Sandra, Doctor Koi smiled as she took Sandra's hand and squeezed it.

"I'm safe up there and I'm safe down here. Don't worry about me, OK?"

"I'll try not to," said Maureen.

"Text me, eh?" said Sandra, handing Maureen a cell phone. "You can use this. Courtesy of Don."

"Aw. That's so sweet." Maureen tucked her new phone into her purse. "Tell him thanks for me."

"Text him yourself. He put his contact info on your phone."

"All right now," Missus Cheffie said. "Listen to me, Maureen. Pay attention. Please don't ever let Xavier know we know? Promise?"

"I promise."

"I think he'd be really embarrassed. He thinks he runs things here on Topside."

Laughter.

"Who's going to be embarrassed?" came a voice from the far end of the shelter. It was Xavier. "What are you guys up to now?"

"Oh, nothing."

"Nope, nothing," echoed everyone else.

"That can't be good." Xavier was at Maureen's side, but he wasn't laughing.

Instead, his eyes were boring into hers. There were no tears in his eyes, not even threatened tears, either in his or hers. But the caring, the respect, the expectations of future meetings were there in abundance.

"Well, dear girl? Are you ready?"

"That I am, dear boy."

"Don't be a stranger."

"I won't."

"Promise?"

"Promise."

They were in each other's arms and their lips were so close to touching, the crowd behind them held its collective breath.

Almost, almost, but...

They stepped away from each other.

The crowd exhaled as one.

"Another time?" said Xavier.

"Text me when."

"Will do, dear girl. Will do."

Acknowledgments

HEARTFELT THANKS TO my editor, Phyllis Bohonis, and my reviewers, Adam Jarvis and Catina Noble.

About the Author

SHERRILL WARK IS a former editor who designs print/digital books for Indie authors. She's the author of: *How to Write a Book: Park It, Get to Work* (non-fiction); *Graven Images* (horror); *Vivie Goes to Hell in a Hatchback* (YA); *Death in l'Acadie: a Kesk8a story*; *Refuge in l'Acadie: a Kesk8a story*; *Trapped in l'Acadie: a Kesk8a story*; and *Hanged for l'Acadie: a Kesk8a story* (historical fiction series, two more to come); and *The Closet Hides a Set of Stairs* (poetry). Under her pseudonym Christina Crowe, she has published *A Girl Dog's Breakfast*, scary stories and rude poems, and *The Unkindest Cut: Short Creepy Movie Scripts*. Sherrill Wark also writes screenplays, one of which, *The Bus to Lo Siento* (drama) landed in the top 10% (out of 600) in the 2013 Oaxaca Film Fest.

www.ingramcontent.com/pod-product-compliance
Lightning Source LLC
Chambersburg PA
CBHW050932120626
46552CB00001B/173